Marsh
7330 Willow Oak Dr
West Bloomfield, MI 48324

MW01265404

SURVIVAL FROM MALICE

Dear Marsha,

Enjoy!

Doreen Lichtman

5-06

SURVIVAL FROM MALICE

▼

Doreen Lichtman

iUniverse, Inc.
New York Lincoln Shanghai

Survival from Malice

iUniverse books may be ordered through booksellers or by contacting:

iUniverse
2021 Pine Lake Road, Suite 100
Lincoln, NE 68512
www.iuniverse.com
1-800-Authors (1-800-288-4677)

Formerly titled: Never The Same

ISBN-13: 978-0-595-36593-7 (pbk)
ISBN-13: 978-0-595-81022-2 (ebk)
ISBN-10: 0-595-36593-0 (pbk)
ISBN-10: 0-595-81022-5 (ebk)

Printed in the United States of America

In Memory of Betty and Nathan, with Love.

PREFACE

It took sixty-nine years for Rebecca Abrom's story to be told. Tom Brokaw's program "Dateline" of January 2, 2004, "Sudden Impact," motivated the author to begin unraveling her mother's past. She thought, *The time was right! The public needed to know the damage inflicted by drunken drivers upon innocent lives.*

Rebecca revealed to her daughters, and then to her grand-daughters, a series of events that involved a childhood surrounded by death. At age nineteen, she found her prince charming, married, and escaped an existence of misery. A year later she had her first-born child and finally had made peace with life. In 1935, however, at age twenty-one, Rebecca became a victim, hit by a drunk driver, and left to die in the street.

This book depicts her trauma and fight to stay alive, save her leg, and endure the consequence—chronic, searing pain.

Hopefully, this story will inform and capture the reader's attention and make clear the strength and fortitude necessary to survive such an ordeal. If reading this book deters a single person from drinking and driving, then Rebecca's sixty-four years of living with pain was not in vain.

ACKNOWLEDGEMENTS

Many thanks to instructor Fran Knorr and classmates in the creative writing class in West Bloomfield, Michigan.

Thanks to Mariette Goldberg, Alice Nigoghosian, and John Nathan for editing the book.

A special thanks to my husband, Irving, for proofreading and giving support, while I spent unlimited hours at the computer.

Thanks to my children, Michelle and David Soble and Lori and Paul Sander, for input and support while writing my book.

CHAPTER 1

▼

SUDDENLY...

The sun burst into Rebecca's bedroom window, coaxing her to wake up, but this morning her eyes were already wide open. She did a long stretch and jumped out of bed, eager to begin the day. Rebecca looked at the clock. Only four more hours before meeting the girls at Millie's house for lunch and playing gin rummy. She was anxious to get out, after being cooped up with a cold for a week, she felt the need for a break from caring for Rena, her one-year-old daughter. Hearing the baby cry, Rebecca knew it was time to get Rena out of bed. "Come on, little one; let's get you dressed and fed. Mommy has much to do before she leaves."

Rena's tears wouldn't stop and she clung to her mother, as if warning her not to go out. Rebecca thought her behavior odd.

"You have no fever or runny nose. Why are you fussing so much? Daddy will be home soon to take care of you."

She gave the baby a cracker to calm her down and placed her in the playpen with some toys. Rebecca scurried to get the house cleaned, and write instructions so Nathan, her husband, would understand what to do for the child. In reality, notes were not needed, because Nathan had cared for Rena since birth. Rebecca was a perfectionist and knowing that he followed her directions gave her a sense of control.

With an hour to get dressed, Rebecca rushed to her closet to select an outfit to wear on this crisp fall day. She knew the worsted wool suit purchased last week from Siegel's specialty shop in downtown Detroit would be perfect. *I know the girls will drool with envy when they see me in the latest style for 1935*, she thought. She looked in the mirror and admired the long slender skirt, designed with the torso of the jacket sensuously molded beneath squared shoulders. The bottom of the jacket floated into a peplum style that tapered to a V-shape tail in the back. To complete the outfit, she wore rounded-toe, chunky heel pumps, a hat slightly tilted at an angle, and carried a black leather pocketbook with matching black gloves. Still admiring her reflection, Rebecca looked satisfied and exclaimed, "Wow!"

Ready to leave, she greeted Nathan as he entered the doorway.

"Hi, honey. There is salami for a sandwich and a salad in the ice box. The baby food is on the kitchen counter. I left you a few notes for Rena's care and Millie's phone number." She called Rena, "Come give mommy a kiss goodbye." The toddler waddled down the hall cautiously, as she had just started walking a month ago. With smiles and giggles, she gave her mother hugs and kisses. "I love you, my sweet child. Mommy will be home after your nap."

Rena was used to her mother going out after her father returned home each morning following his work as a baker on the night shift. Father and daughter enjoyed their special time. They always ate lunch together and played until nap time for both of them. Nathan had not slept since the previous day.

Rebecca finished applying her makeup and then quickly peeked in the living room to watch her husband and Rena play their silly games and sing funny songs. "One, two—I see you. Three, four—Let's play more." A smile beamed across Rebecca's face as she thought to herself: *How lucky I am to have Nathan home to help, so I'm free to run errands, meet friends, and do volunteer work.* She looked at her watch. *Oh, I better hurry or I'll be late to Millie's.* "Goodbye," she yelled, and ran out the door.

As Rebecca walked six blocks to her friend's house, she took in the splendors of autumn with the changing colors of the leaves in hues of yellows and reds, while she inhaled the freshness of the brisk day. She approached busy Clairmont Avenue with streetcars running in both directions. There were no traffic signals on the corner and Rebecca didn't feel like going to the end of the block to cross at the light. However, a pedestrian island lined Clairmount to increase the safety of people crossing. Once across, Millie's house was only a block away. Rebecca walked to the island and waited for clearance to approach the other side. Suddenly, like a bolt of lightning, a car rushed towards her, knocking her down. As Rebecca fell, the tail of her suit jacket caught onto the car's bumper and she was dragged along the streetcar tracks. Shocked by the rapid change of events, she panicked. *What's happening to me? I'm going to die. Oh God, I don't want to leave my baby and husband.* Rebecca felt her leg's skin tearing open, blood dripping down, and the metal tracks scorching the wounds as her body was jostled by the speed of the car. "Save me! Save me!" She shrieked and lost consciousness. Finally, after the car hit a bump, the jacket released and Rebecca hit the ground. The black car sped away.

Because Clairmount was a thoroughfare, it was heavily populated with people traveling in every direction. While waiting for a bus, Ray Simon heard screams. He looked up and saw the accident. He quickly yelled for others to come and help.

One man shouted, "Don't move her! You might injure her more."

A woman cried, "Call an ambulance. Call the police."

Traffic moved fast and Mr. Simon feared that another car might hit the young woman. He directed others to lift and carefully place her body at curbside. Rebecca was still unconscious and oblivious to the commotion around her.

With the sirens screaming, a Calvert Company Ambulance weaved in and out of traffic towards the accident. The location was hard to pinpoint, as the woman who gave the information was hysterical. "Quick, come, a lady was hit by a speeding car," was all she had told them.

The medics responding to the call feared the worst. They approached the corner where a crowd had gathered. Bill, the driver, saw a motionless body lying face up. He remarked to his partner, Max, "It looks like we have a corpse to bring to the morgue."

As they made their way through the crowd, Bill and Max saw a young woman sprawled on the cement. The picture looked bleak. Bill's lunch began to surface on the roof of his mouth and left a foul taste; but he managed to swallow it back down.

"Bill, the girl looks barely twenty."

Max could tell she was nicely dressed, even though her suit was torn and covered in blood. Scratches and cuts covered her milky white skin, but what held the medics' attention was her right leg: ripped open, with nerves, muscles and tendons dangling like spaghetti. Bill bent down to take her pulse and found a faint response. He yelled to Max, "She's still alive. We have to get her to the hospital fast."

Bill quickly wrapped the leg and covered the victim in a blanket. The police, who arrived on the scene just after the ambulance, redirected traffic and held back the gathering crowd. Bill and Max transferred the body onto a stretcher, took their seats, and headed for Receiving Hospital, with sirens screaming. Officer McQuire questioned the onlookers to find witnesses to the accident. Ray Simon was the first to step forward. "It was terrible. The poor lady didn't have a chance," he said.

"Just tell me what you saw. Did you get a look at the car or catch the license number?"

"The car was black. Um, no, dark green or maybe dark blue. I can't remember. It happened so fast and I was more concerned about the woman than the driver." At age seventy-seven, Simon felt tired, his heart weak, and unprepared for such stress.

"I'm sorry, officer; the car was zigzagging so fast down Clairmount, I just can't be sure. I can't believe the person didn't stop. He probably was drunk."

McQuire jotted down the information and thanked Simon for his cooperation. As the officer turned to look for other witnesses, a young woman in her thirties stepped up.

"I saw the runaway car and caught the first two letters of the license plate." He quickly took Claire Bolton's report, hoping to get as many details as possible. Apologetically, she rambled on about the runaway car being black and all she caught was "LP" of the license. The officer completed his report and asked Mr. Simon and Miss Bolton to stay in town in case they were needed to testify in court at a later date. Bolton nervously twirled the fringes of her scarf, fearing the idea of facing the public. Anger took over, however, and she forced out the courageous words: "Don't worry, officer; I'll be around if you need my help. Just find the jerk that left that poor girl lying in the street to die."

McQuire started to look for information to identify the victim. He went back to where Mr. Simon said she was hit. On the ground, smashed and cut, he noticed a fine leather pocketbook. A few feet away, he found one shoe and, some distance down the street, he spotted its mate. After looking over the items, McQuire guessed the lady wasn't hurting for money. He collected all the evidence and searched her purse for identification. In a black wallet, McQuire found a card with the name Rebecca

Abrom, an address, and phone number. Her birth date was October 26, 1914. He shook his head thinking: *This girl is only twenty-one years old. I sure hope she makes it. This is one visit to inform the family I dread making.*

McQuire knew that with so little evidence, the investigation would quickly fall apart, unless something developed with the letters "LP." As he approached his squad car, he turned and recognized Ron Spector, the flamboyant *Detroit Times* reporter.

"Spector, if you came sniffing around here for a story, good luck! You won't find enough information to go on."

CHAPTER 2

▼

THE INVESTIGATION

It was 1:00 p.m. when Raymond Miller, Jr. skidded into the garage of his parents' home on Boston Boulevard. Their house stood stately on a deep lot facing an evenly maple-treed avenue with manicured shrubs and lawns encompassing the neighborhood. He entered the side door, finding his mother busy in the library planning the fund-raising campaign for her husband's reelection to City Council.

"Mother, I need to talk to you right away."

Raymond was shaking as he entered the library. His ashen white face had tears streaming down.

"What happened to you?"

His mother had never seen her son in such a state.

"I think I did a terrible thing. I hit something on the road. It dragged on the back of my car and then broke loose. I was too frightened to get out of the car to check it out."

"You mean too drunk," muttered his mother. "Calm down and tell me exactly what happened."

"I was traveling west on Clairmount, after only three drinks at Pete's Tavern. I swear I wasn't drunk, but probably driving a little too fast. Then I hit something and heard screams. My car lagged and then regained its speed. I drove away without looking back."

"Maybe you hit an animal and it caught underneath your car and then fell off."

"I don't know. I just don't know."

Raymond was agitated and Mrs. Miller knew it was time to call her husband to get instruction on how to proceed with this matter. She dialed his private office number, and after four rings, was about to hang up, when Mr. Miller finally whispered "hello." He was in a meeting and didn't appreciate being disturbed. Yet, when he heard his wife's hysterics over something his son did, he knew he had to end the meeting and come home to see what trouble Raymond was in. He gave his secretary a nervous look.

"I'll be back in a couple of hours. Any calls, tell them I'm in a meeting."

Betsy Conner knew never to question Councilman Miller's directions when he left the office abruptly. He retrieved his car from valet and drove toward Boston Boulevard. Mr. Miller reflected on how many times he had come to his son's rescue. Problems with Raymond started early. He was teased at school and got into fights out of anger. By age twenty-two, Raymond used alcohol regularly.

But Mr. Miller was too busy building his career to attend to Raymond's issues and Mrs. Miller was at her husband's side helping to bolster his political aspirations. It was easier for the Millers to find excuses or get him off the hook with payoffs and favors. Raymond was stopped many times for drunk driving, but the cases were never pursued, thanks to Councilman Miller's political status. It was an election year and Miller knew his career was at stake if his son's behavior reached the press. As Miller approached the house, a nauseous feeling attacked his stomach. *What did my son do today that was so awful?* Raymond was sitting in the library waiting for his father. As Mr. Miller approached, he saw a fear in his son's eyes that he had never seen before. He sat down in his favorite leather chair to listen patiently. Raymond repeated the story he had already told his mother and waited for his father's reaction.

"So you really don't know what you hit or if you hit anything?"

"I know I hit something, but I don't know what. I'm really scared, dad. What can I do? I should have stopped, I know that..."

"But you were too drunk." His father tried to control his temper. Raymond looked down with shame. He knew he never could live up to his father's expectations.

"I'm sorry; I just can't stop drinking. I know I'm a disappointment to you and mother. I don't know what to do."

His father spoke sharply. "I'll tell you what I'm going to do. I'll go to the police station and inquire about any reported accidents. If you were involved in one in anyway, I will help you out of this jam, but it will be the last time. You will quietly leave this city and never return. I will not put my future in jeopardy over your stupidity. I know a doctor, out-of-state, who can help you discreetly with your drinking problem. Refuse treatment and you are on your own. Flounder around without direction and you'll amount to nothing."

Raymond sat silent. He had never seen his father in such a mood and knew that this wasn't the time to challenge his decision.

"I'll make this up to you dad; I swear I will."

"Yeah, yeah; these promises are old hat. I'm leaving for the police station. Stay put until I return and I forbid you to drive your car."

Mr. Miller rushed out of the house without speaking or reassuring his wife. She looked out the window with apprehension.

Officer McQuire knocked on the Abroms' front door to inform the family about the accident, but no one answered. He returned to the police station to finish his report and hand it to Detective Pierce, who was assigned to the investigation. If the victim should die, the case would become a homicide and that was Pierce's expertise. McQuire started to walk towards Pierce with the paperwork, when Councilman Miller entered and moved towards them.

"Hello, gentlemen; I came to see Captain Brooks about a matter. Oh, by the way, I hear a serious accident occurred this afternoon."

McQuire and Pierce looked at each other puzzled, and wondered how Miller got the news so fast. *What was his interest in today's accident?* They knew he regularly came around asking for favors, especially for his son, and they obliged, knowing that he and the captain were close friends. McQuire spoke up:

"There was a hit-and-run at Clairmount and Linwood at 12:30 p.m. today." Miller felt his body stiffen and was afraid to ask the next question.

"How serious was it?"

"Pretty serious. The victim was taken to Receiving in a coma after being dragged on the streetcar tracks about seventy-five feet. We have some information on the car and license number, but it may not be enough. Let's hope she survives. Do you have a personal interest in this case?" Pierce sensed something was wrong.

Miller's legs were ready to buckle from weakness and he felt the room spinning. He thought, *If they acquire the license number, my son's life is doomed and my career is over.* He tried to regain his composure and exit the room fast. He backed out toward the door.

"Thanks for the information, fellows. I overheard some talk around the office and was concerned. See you around."

Miller's shirt was damp from sweat and he felt his heart palpitating. He went to turn the door knob to leave, when a voice called him.

"Captain Brooks is available to see you now, Councilman Miller."

Miller froze on the spot. He took a deep breath and turned to give Jenny, the Captain's secretary, a nod. He opened the door slowly and greeted his friend with a handshake.

"What brings you here in the middle of the afternoon, Ray?"

"I just came to say hello, while in the neighborhood. As I was waiting to see you, McQuire and Pierce filled me in on the tragic accident that happened this afternoon on Clairmount."

Somberly, Brooks replied, "I hate a hit-and-run accident. No arrest, no conviction, no compensation for the victim. Hopefully, the woman survives without complications."

"I hear you have a license number and description of the car."

"Nah, we have only two letters of the plate and maybe the color of the car. Truthfully, with this little information, it's too costly to pursue the case."

"I agree that putting your budget in jeopardy over this wouldn't make you too popular with the mayor."

"You're right about that, Ray. I'll give Pierce a week to look into the accident. If nothing comes up, file closed."

Miller felt a bit relieved, and hoped Brooks didn't notice his beads of sweat and shaky hands. As Miller approached the door to leave, he turned to Brooks:

"What were the two letters on the license plate retrieved from the witness?"

"LP on a black car."

Miller felt sick again. Raymond's plate number was LP 173. His car was black.

"What was the victim's name?"

Brooks looked a little surprised, "Rebecca Abrom, age 21."

Miller felt the blood draining from his body.

"Is she married?"

"We think so. McQuire found a picture of a little girl in her pocketbook, but when he went to the house to notify the family, no one answered. He's going back at about 3:00 p.m."

Brooks glanced suspiciously at Miller. "Why all the questions, Ray? Is something bothering you about this case?" Brooks thought about Miller's son and wondered if he had something to do with the accident. Raymond Miller, Jr. didn't have a good track record.

"No. The woman is a constituent and I was concerned, that's all."

The pain in Miller's stomach felt like acid chomping away at the lining, heading towards the esophagus, and coming up the throat leaving a sour taste. *Where is my ulcer medication? I better leave before Brooks starts to put ideas together.* He swiftly opened the door, waved goodbye, and let himself out without looking back.

Miller hit the pavement hard and fast with an urgency to reach his office and start planning for Raymond's departure. As a councilman, Ray had connections and activating a scheme wouldn't be difficult. Miller put his thoughts in order. *First, the car needs to disappear to abolish any evidence, and the license plate must be destroyed. Secondly, I need to find a sanatorium to help Raymond stop drinking and deal with his anger. Finally, I'll call my contact, Bruce Styles, to get the ball rolling.* He closed the door to his office and spoke softly to Bruce on the phone,

"Raymond must leave now, before the police start their investigation. His drunk driving record and license plate number make him a prime suspect. It's my political clout that keeps him out of jail."

Miller hung up and buried his head in his hands. *Am I doing the right thing by sending him away? Even if the woman survives, my son still needs help. One semester left to complete college, but no interest in school. Grades are down and he looks for excuses to hang out with drinking buddies. Minor auto accidents are a norm until today's catastrophe. My son is angry and resentful. I can no longer ignore or wish away the problems.*

Before leaving the office, Miller called Receiving Hospital to inquire on Mrs. Abrom's condition. The nursing station reported that she was in serious condition, but off the critical list. He felt relieved and thought maybe this story wouldn't end tragically. He had never seen his son so shaken up over anything before, but he decided not to give him the hospital report. *Let him be scared enough to leave Detroit. Maybe this is his last chance to get and stay sober and begin his life over.*

When Miller arrived home that evening, he called his son and wife together to discuss the events of the day and explain what he had learned at the police station.

• "Margaret, Detective Pierce has information about the case that may implicate Raymond. We don't know if the woman he hit will survive. I initiated a plan for our son to leave town and receive treatment for his binge drinking. No investigation, no chance of a trial or going to jail if found guilty."

"Son, you will leave for New York tomorrow on the 9:00 a.m. train. A driver will be waiting to transport you to the Rosemont clinic in Riverdale. It's about an hour outside

Manhattan. Dr. Harold Debrinski, a leading psychiatrist and the clinic director, is going to treat you."

Mrs. Miller wept and Raymond kept his head down without saying a word. He knew he couldn't get out of this mess without his father's help. Ray looked at his wife with compassion, but spoke firmly.

"We can't protect him any longer, Margaret. He has to help himself to end this nightmare."

He grabbed his son and gave him a hug, something he hadn't done for a long while. Tears swelled in his eyes. Raymond couldn't remember the last time his father showed him any affection and he stood stiffly, not knowing how to return this gesture. His father backed away. "I will support you until the treatment is over. Then you will find a job and learn to survive on your own. Please write us and let us know how you are doing, but there is no coming home for a very long time."

Raymond, Jr. had empathy for the woman he hit, but he couldn't let it ruin his life. He felt remorse, but going to prison wasn't an option. This time he would cooperate with his parents, but he resented going to the clinic. In his mind, Raymond denied being an alcoholic and believed he just needed a break to get on with his life. *I know my father is more concerned over his career than my welfare, but I don't want his career ruined over my negligence. Maybe going to New York will be a new adventure. After awhile, I'll dump the clinic and move to the city and see what opportunities await me.*

CHAPTER 3

▼

THE HOSPITAL

Officer McQuire and Detective Pierce arrived at the Abrom house around 3:00 p.m. Nathan and Rena, up from their nap, were playing "roll the ball," while waiting for Rebecca to return. The doorbell rang and Nathan wondered why Becky didn't use her key. Nathan looked out the window and saw two strangers standing outside. He opened the door to inquire what they wanted. Pierce presented his badge and asked if he could come in.

"Sure. Come in; have a seat."

"Mr. Abrom," Pierce said, "Is Rebecca Abrom related to you?"

"Yes: She's my wife. What happened to her? She's supposed to be home by now."

"I'm sorry to inform you that your wife was involved in a bad accident. She was hit by a car at around 12:30 p.m., while crossing Clairmount. She was rushed to Receiving Hospital."

"How bad is she?" Nathan quivered, as his heart palpitated.

"Presently, she's out of a coma, but we don't know the extent of her injuries. We tried contacting you earlier. There was no answer."

Nathan thought he had heard a noise at the door, but put it out of his mind as he was trying to fall asleep. *How could I be so stupid not to investigate?*

"Please," he begged the officers, "take me to my wife. Wait here. I'll see if my neighbor can watch my daughter."

Nathan ran to Mrs. Posner's apartment with Rena in his arms. He quickly explained what happened and begged Mrs. Posner to take her until he arrived home from the hospital. Lillian Posner reassured Nathan.

"Don't worry. I'll take good care of your little girl. Just go and see how Becky is doing. Heaven forbid something bad happens to her."

Nathan, bent down on one knee, explained to his daughter that he needed to go find Mommy and would come home soon. She smiled and waved goodbye. Rena liked visiting the Posners, because of their three and six-year-old daughters, and oh-so-many toys.

With neighbors' eyes probing, Nathan got into the police car. Sirens placed the car ahead of traffic as they sped toward the hospital. He worried his wife was suffering and was frightened over the nightmare that might await him. His tense body felt sweaty and clammy. *I have to stay strong for my family. I can't let them see desperation.* As they approached the majestic red brick building, Nathan stood afraid. But the white marble gothic columns surrounding the entrance gave the illusion of strength and power. As they pulled the mighty doors open, Nathan felt calmness radiate from within the building. His confidence surged and he told himself, *Becky will survive.*

"Help me; please someone help me," Rebecca cried.

She awoke, startled by her surroundings. Her pain was paralyzing. A nurse came running to try and calm her down as she continued her ramblings. The nurse ran for a doctor. Dr. Kirk administered a shot of morphine and soon Rebecca fell into a stupor. Kathy, her nurse, understood the torment the patient endured. She had been on duty when the medics brought her in. Kathy remembered the blood-soaked bandages wrapped around her leg. As the doctor cut them away to treat the wound, she felt nauseous looking at the semblance of a leg. The talk around the floor was that the leg would need amputation. Dr. Kirk washed Rebecca's leg with sulfur to avoid infection and wrapped it. He turned to Kathy in an urgent tone.

"Why isn't any family here yet? We need some medical decisions made on what to do with this leg."

The two officers and Nathan ran up the stairs and through the double doors to reach the reception area. They inquired about Rebecca and were escorted to a room on the second floor. As they approached the medical area, they heard screams. Tears swelled in Nathan's eyes. He knew their ordeal had begun. He ran to the room and found his wife tied down to keep her from thrashing around from intense pain. He grabbed her hand. She looked up crying and rambling.

"Where am I? What happened? What are they doing to me? The pain is unbearable."

Questions were flowing faster then Nathan could answer. Rebecca was shaking from torment, fear, and the unknown.

"Calm down, honey. I'll try to explain what happened to you."

Dr. Kirk heard the patient's husband had finally arrived and came in the room to introduce himself and explain Rebecca's medical condition.

"We took X-rays and contacted an orthopedic doctor. He concluded that Mrs. Abrom's leg was crushed and needs amputating as soon as possible. We're afraid gangrene will set in and take over her body. The infection will kill her."

When Rebecca heard her leg must come off, she started screaming: "No, no. I'll kill you if you take off my leg."

Nathan was having a hard time grasping all the information and listening to his wife's agony. He told Dr. Kirk, "I need to speak to the surgeon before we can decide what to do. My wife is only twenty-one; how can I let them cut off her leg?"

Dr. Kirk was sympathetic to the Abroms, but felt they had no choice.

"I'll call Dr. Kopel to come speak with you, but we need to make a decision soon."

Officers McQuire and Pierce left the room vowing to find the person responsible.

Dr. Kopel arrived at Rebecca's room to explain the procedure to be used for the operation.

"If I amputate and leave enough of a stump to wear an artificial leg, Rebecca could learn to walk again with a slight limp."

Rebecca was crying hysterically and Nathan felt helpless. He pulled the doctor aside and pleaded,

"Aren't there any other options? I beg you; please try to save her leg. At her age, how can she accept this fate? She has a whole life ahead of her."

Dr. Kopel thought a moment and then hesitantly said, "There is an option, but I can't promise any miracles and we have to hurry with a decision. There is an orthopedic surgeon that works on difficult cases. He's your only hope, but he's very expensive and takes only private pay."

Nathan looked up with a spark of hope. "I don't care what it costs or how hard I have to work to pay the bills."

Dr. Kopel replied, "I'll contact Dr. Palmer immediately and tell him it's urgent."

Dr. Palmer arrived late that afternoon to review the scenario. He found the X-rays fascinating and knew the case posed a challenge. *If I mend her leg and make it functional, the surgery could make me famous. I'd present it to my colleagues at seminars and write it up in medical journals. The publicity could be endless.*

Relief came when Dr. Palmer told the Abroms he would perform the operation. Nathan promised that he would pay whatever it cost.

"Don't worry about money right now; we'll work everything out."

Rebecca and Nathan listened intently to this self-assured doctor.

"The surgery will take about eight to ten hours depending on how difficult it will be to reconnect tissue. I'll use my discretion on the hardware needed to hold her leg together. You'll be in the hospital with a cast for about a year. When the cast comes off, you'll need a brace for walking, but hopefully, with therapy and time, you will walk without assistance. The risk is infection or that the leg won't hold together. However, if the surgery works, you must promise never to abuse the leg by overuse."

Rebecca listened, but only heard the words "walk again." Nathan assessed the risks and felt fear and apprehension. *His wife's life was in Palmer's hands. Was this young doctor capable of such complicated surgery? Did he have the right credentials?* Rebecca was sure he was the right surgeon for the job, and his confidence helped her make the decision. She felt there was no choice.

"I want to keep my leg and he is the one to save it. Okay, Dr. Palmer, schedule the operation and get it done."

Nathan kept silent.

"Surgery will be scheduled for tomorrow morning. Our time is running out. Mr. Abrom, make arrangements with the hospital administrator for payment. Their bill is separate from mine."

Palmer left the hospital without trepidation. As a German soldier in World War I, he witnessed mangled legs, lost limbs, and battered bodies. His salvation from the sorrow of war was to learn the art of healing, but he had to leave Hamburg, Germany to attain his goals. Politics and government there started to move in a direction that frightened him. In America he achieved his medical ambitions. He selected Detroit because of supportive relatives who arrived during the 1900's. He arrived in Detroit in 1920 and attended City College and Detroit College of Medicine. By age thirty-six, he had completed orthopedic training at the University of Michigan and studied surgical techniques through the Clinical Congress of Surgeons. He opened an office in the Penobscot Building in downtown Detroit and performed surgery out of Receiving and Harper Hospitals. His surgeries and successes escalated. His name became well-known within the medical arena.

Palmer returned to his office after seeing the Abroms and started drawing a diagram of the leg and planning what he needed to do to reconstruct it. He had one night to think through the procedure. *Am I promising these people too much? Repairing broken bones is one thing, but putting together a mangled leg is a different story.* However, the prospect of the glory if successful outweighed the fear of failure. He fumbled through the office storage room looking for materials usable for pinning the patient's leg together. Disappointed, Palmer traveled to the nearest hardware store. He looked for different types of metal plates, screws, and bolts, wondering which would fit into the leg and anchor it. Dr. Palmer's reputation was built on his willingness to use unorthodox techniques. If the standard orthopedic supplies didn't work, a little innovation was needed. *Rebecca Abrom didn't need to know what was placed inside her leg, as long as it held together and she could walk,* believed Palmer. He proceeded to buy the necessary items required for surgery. The next morning, he had the surgical nurse sterilize the hardware in boiling water to prepare for the procedure.

Miss Decker, Overseer of Hospital Operations, sat in her office waiting to meet with Nathan Abrom at 3:00 p.m. on the day before his wife's operation. Decker was aware of the implications of this case. From the information she gathered about the accident and how much care would be needed for this patient, she had to carefully figure the cost of keeping Mrs. Abrom for one year. Hospitals suffered from the depression. The demand for free care rose while patients' incomes declined. Receiving, however, was a subsidized hospital. Mr. Abrom explained his case to Miss Decker after introducing himself and taking a seat in her office,

"I'm an established baker at Sander's Bakery and Confectionary. Unlike most people still recuperating from the crash of 1929 and depression, I work, earn a decent salary, and survived with financial stability. I was never unemployed and made good money through the years. My investments were in bonds."

"Now is the time to sell your assets," advised Miss Decker. "You'll need your savings and a portion of your salary for your wife's care. You will be responsible for $2500 of the cost and your surgeon will bill you separately. Since we are a non-profit, voluntary hospital, you are responsible for a portion of the cost. The balance will be covered by government funding."

Nathan knew he would be financially wiped out. His only hope was that the police find the driver who was responsible for the destruction of their lives and that compensation might ensue. But Nathan couldn't rely on that fantasy.

"I'll find a second job to survive, but I need to find someone to care for my child," he said.

Miss Decker sympathized with Nathan Abrom's predicament, but she had a job to do. "Your wife will receive excellent care here and your money will buy her a semi-private room instead of a ward," she reassured Nathan. "Good luck on her surgery tomorrow."

Nathan stood up, shook Miss Decker's hand, thanked her for the help, and walked out. He rushed to Rebecca's room to comfort her and to tell her not to worry about expenses.

"I worked everything out, Rebecca; the government will pay for most of the bill," Nathan lied.

Rebecca nodded with approval, but was groggy from sedation. She extended her hand to grab Nathan.

"Please take care of Rena," she begged.

Then she fell asleep. Nathan sat down and rested his head near Rebecca's arm. This medical crisis brought pounding and pressure to his head. Thoughts spun out of control. *Can I keep our family glued together? Who will take care of Rena while I work a second job to pay the bills?* A voice went off inside his head: *Run, get your bonds, and disappear. Never,* thought Nathan. *I'll take care of my family at any cost.* Nathan leaned over and kissed Rebecca goodnight. He walked out of the hospital in search of answers.

Nathan picked up Rena at the Posners' house and tried to explain the outcome of this afternoon's tragic event. Mrs. Posner was sympathetic and offered to give some assistance. He thanked her and took Rena home to eat dinner. He didn't have much of an appetite. He managed to swallow a salami sandwich and fed his daughter Gerber mashed sweet potatoes and beef stew. She smacked her lips over the vanilla pudding. Getting Rena ready for bed was the easiest task. Calling relatives and friends explaining about the accident and inquiring as to who could care for his child was difficult. Finally, relief came when Aunt Sophie offered temporary help, but a more permanent arrangement was needed. Nathan scheduled a new person each week so no one individual was burdened. He tried his hardest to keep Rebecca's stepmother from caring for Rena, because of her resentment towards his wife, but it didn't work. He needed her. The list of caretakers ran out.

CHAPTER 4

▼

CRITICAL HOURS

Nathan came early on the morning of surgery and went to wish his wife good luck. They kept her sedated, but she recognized Nathan and waved to him. At 7:00 o'clock, two orderlies came for Rebecca. They transferred her onto a gurney and started to wheel her towards surgery. "Wait," yelled Nathan. He ran down the hall and gave Rebecca one last kiss. "I'll be here waiting for you, sweetie."

He didn't know if he would see or talk to his wife again. He didn't want to leave her side, but the nurse escorted him into the waiting room. Nathan sat down and tilted his head back trying to doze. He knew it would be a long day. The antiseptic stench within the perimeters of the walls filled his nostrils and he found it hard to be comfortable. His mind wandered. *Even if the surgery were successful and Rebecca walked again, their life would never be the same.* How much of a change remained unknown. Then Nathan fell asleep.

Rebecca was lying in a cold, white, sterile room with bright lights reflecting off the ceiling. A mask was placed on her face and she started to feel sleepy. The ether was having its effect. Rebecca was out. Dr. Palmer and his surgical staff proceeded. They undid the bandages. As Palmer looked at the leg, he knew time was running out. He needed to get in quickly, to repair and suture before bacteria set in. The procedure was long and tedious. Palmer's agile and skilled hands patiently threaded together the leg's network of inner fibers, like a spider meticulously weaving his web. Nurse Kathy kept wiping the sweat from his brow, as he labored with the plate and screws. Blood spurted and Becky's hemoglobin dropped. A blood transfusion was needed fast.

"Let's hook up some blood," yelled the resident.

Going into the eighth hour, Palmer was finally ready for casting. He worked with his team to finalize the long and intense surgery. When it was completed, he took off his surgical gloves, gave a sigh of relief and said, "Let us pray."

Nathan woke from his nap and paced the floor waiting to hear the results. Friends and relatives visited to help ease the agony of the long day. Some donated blood to replenish the bank. This kept the hospital from charging for Rebecca's transfusion. Doctor Palmer found Nathan in the waiting room talking with family when he came to inform him of the outcome.

"I think it was successful, but only time will tell."

Finally, Rebecca was wheeled to her room. Nathan ran to her side. She felt in another world until the anesthesia wore off. Wearily, she inquired, "How did it go?"

"Dr. Palmer thinks it went well, but it's going to take a long time before he knows if he truly succeeded."

He stayed with her a while and then left to get Rena. Rebecca fell back asleep. Darkness seeped through the window as she woke again. She felt a drawing sensation in the leg from the plaster drying on the cast. She wanted to rip off the cast to relieve the pressure and pain. As Rebecca yelled out in agony, she yearned for the comfort of her mother. *Mom, come hold my hand. I need to see your smile, hear your voice saying you love me like you did when I was a child.* But she knew it was an impossible dream.

CHAPTER 5

▼

REBECCA (JOHNSTOWN TO DETROIT) 1926-1934

Rebecca Hooberman raced home from school on this chilly fall day anxious to tell her mother that Bobby Dinkens pulled her braids again in penmanship class and whispered, "Baby Becky cries 'boo hoo Hooberman.'"

I hate him, thought Rebecca, as she opened the front door to her house and ran upstairs to look for her mother in bed. For the past month, that was her only peaceful haven. Quickly, Rebecca's mind changed from Dinkens' shenanigans to her mother's declining health. She had watched her mother slowly turn into a frail old lady. Her face showed more wrinkles, fat disappeared, and her pallid skin sagged. Her brown starry eyes bulged from their sockets like an owl on night patrol. Mama was only thirty-two years old, but she looked as if her energy was ebbing away.

Rebecca overheard her mother tell Aunt Gertie that the breast cancer was spreading, but Rebecca thought mama meant she had a chest cold that wouldn't go away. She opened the bedroom door and started to explain her story, but abruptly stopped talking. Mama's bed was empty. *That's strange,* she thought.

"Mama, where are you?"

Rebecca looked everywhere upstairs, than hurried downstairs to continue the search. Voices reverberated from the dining room. Rebecca opened the French doors a crack to take a peek. Her eyes widened and her mouth opened with a gasp waiting to come out, but she placed her hand tightly over her mouth to keep the sound from erupting.

Women were bent over her mother, whose body was placed on the dining room table. Her ash-white skeletal figure lay still, while being carefully washed, as prayers were chanted over her body. Mother's favorite dress was spread out and Rebecca noticed a wooden box resting in the corner of the room. Tears swelled up in her eyes like a gale force. She wanted to run as fast as possible. *I can't breathe. I need to get out of here.* Suddenly, she felt a heavy hand touch her shoulder. She quickly turned and saw her father. His red swollen eyes told the story. This was the saddest day of her life.

"Rebecca, your mother died this morning. These women are performing the Holy Society's role. They purify and prepare the body for burial according to Jewish ritual law. They will be here all night watching over the body. Tomorrow is the funeral and then we will sit the customary Shiva, seven days of mourning. After that, I will need your help with raising your sister, Lilly, and little Jakie. I don't need to worry about your brother, Benny. He's old enough to look out for himself."

Then her papa walked away. She wanted to scream, *who's going to care for me? I'm only twelve.* He was gone. Rebecca ran upstairs to her bedroom, placed her head in the pillow, and let the floodgates open. She realized that no one cared.

For seven days, Rebecca sat in a room with people coming and going. Some she knew, others were strangers. Her body felt numb and tense. She heard scrambled words, but couldn't maintain a conversation. She politely said, "Hello," answered "yes" or "no," but her thoughts were with her mother at the cemetery. The image of the casket being lowered into the ground and the Holy Society people throwing dirt over it kept her mesmerized.

After the cakes and cookies were gone and people stopped coming, Rebecca was left with only memories and responsibilities. Two weeks later her anger erupted. Rebecca wanted to go over to her best friend Lucy's house, but couldn't because she had her siblings to care for, a house to clean, and meals to prepare. Fed-up, she started screaming, "Why did you leave me, mama? What did I do that was so bad?"

Soon, Rebecca noticed her father coming home less and less and she became more and more resentful. If she inquired, he shrugged his shoulders and said he had things to do, but he never said why and didn't show much affection toward his family. Rebecca didn't want to anger him. She feared he also might go away. One evening, father brought home a lady to meet the children. Her name was Bertha and Rebecca thought her name seemed to fit her girth. She was buxom, with a laugh that lit up her face. She pinched their cheeks as she said how nice it was to meet the Hooberman kids. About a week later, she came again with hugs and kisses and plenty of gifts, like a tribal peace offering. But an eerie feeling came over Rebecca, who was wise beyond her years. She thought: *This woman is coming into our lives too soon. My prayers for relief are being answered too fast. Mama hasn't even been dead a year and already father is having her replaced. How could he? I know he doesn't know what to do with us, but I thought I was taking care of everything.*

A week later, father and Bertha showed up with their arms intertwined, laughing up a storm, and announced their marriage.

"Children, I want you to be happy and go on with your life without so many burdens."

However, what father didn't know was that their nightmare was just beginning. Bertha moved in that evening without too many parcels except for one big surprise and that was her son, Henry.

Rebecca and Henry became friends, since they were only two years apart. They enjoyed the same music and books, but Bertha didn't like seeing them spend too much time together, as she thought Henry was worthy of spending time with the upper crust of Johnstown, Pennsylvania. She pushed him in the direction of the wealthy Pollick family, whose father was not only a banker but owned thoroughbred horses and a riding stable.

Rebecca had little time to develop or retain friendships, especially during the next four years, when Bertha gave birth to three more children. This brought turmoil to the combined families. Bertha's feelings were divided between hers and the first Mrs. Hooberman's children. So she treated hers like steak and the others like mashed potatoes. Her pinches left welts and the screaming and demands increased.

"Rebecca, this floor needs washing. Why do I have to keep telling you the little ones need baths? Can't you see their dirt? You're lazy, a good-for-nothing. Keep your brother, Jakie, away from me. He's always running around the house."

Father's work on the Pennsylvania Railroad kept him busy and he never questioned Bertha's disciplinarian tactics. Rebecca quit school to help take care of all the kids, while Bertha gallivanted with friends. Henry aligned himself with Rebecca, because he felt abandoned by his mother. The new siblings took all of Bertha's attention.

On a brilliant sunny day in May, Henry approached Rebecca to join him and his best friend, Robert, for an afternoon of horseback riding. Henry had been riding for two years and wanted to show off to Rebecca how good he was. Rebecca declined, as she needed to take Richie for his one-and-a-half-year check-up. No one else was home to watch Rona and Sammy, so they were also her responsibility.

"You work harder than anyone else around this house. You need to have some fun," suggested Henry. "Go, go," urged Rebecca as she shooed him out the door. She knew she couldn't get out of this job no matter how much she wanted to join him.

The phone rang late that afternoon and Rebecca thought it was Bertha calling to say she was detained and to inquire about Richie's appointment. However, the hysterics on the other end alarmed her. She heard Robert explain while sobbing, "Henry's horse got spooked by a car horn and started galloping so hard that he lost control and was thrown from the horse and broke his neck. Henry died instantly."

Rebecca froze on the spot and the phone dropped from her hand. She started to move, but her knees caved in. She screamed, "How could this happen? He was my support, my friend, and now he is gone. I feel so alone."

Benny, her oldest sibling, had left to join the Army. Now Rebecca was the oldest and in charge of five children. Desperate, she needed relief, but none came. To keep sane, she escaped to her bedroom at night and entered in a journal the feelings that tormented her. It later became a secret poem:

My head rests on my pillow.
I'm sad from my thoughts.
How do I continue
Dealing with my loss?

I need help.
I'm feeling so alone.
My mother died.
My father's seldom home.

I'm called upon to cook and bake.
To care for one sister
And my brother, Jake.

My siblings won't listen,
When I tell them what to do.
They act angry, they pout and are rude.

I'm only twelve and my heart is
Trying to mend from the death of
My mother, my friend.

I need help.
I'm so tired.
I just want to be free.
I try to attend school,
Then quickly return home.
That is the rule.

Please help me.
No one is aware of how
I try to keep my family together.
Instead of being torn apart.
That would break my heart.
One night, my dad came home,
But he was not alone. He brought
A strange woman, who changed
The family's tone.

He called her his wife and
Explained how she would
Change our life. But this
Devious woman showed her might.

After five years of marriage,
Came three more mouths to feed.
Now, I cook, clean, and take care of five.
My adolescence gone, I want to die.

I can't escape this drudgery.
Too young to be on my own.
No school, few friends, no fun.
My work is never done.

Please help me God.
I know you are there.
Hear my prayers.
Let someone, somehow, someway,
Come and take me away.

Bertha stayed locked in her room and wailed for weeks after the funeral. When she finally decided to rejoin the human race, she became more resentful then ever. One of her steaks had perished, while the mashed potatoes lingered on. So when Jakie mouthed back at Bertha, "I won't clean the cellar. I'm afraid to go down there alone. It's dark and scary," Bertha went berserk.

Her face transformed into the look of the devil returning from hell. Her glaring eyes burned like fire and her mouth formed a crooked grimace as words of filth spewed out.

"You ass. Why are you alive, while my son is dead?" Her arm lashed out and grabbed Jakie by surprise. She opened the cellar door and pushed him down the stairs. The children watched, but no one was going to speak up and deal with her wrath. Rebecca brushed past Bertha in a rush to reach her brother. Her worst fear was that he was dead. When she reached the cellar floor, she heard his cries of pain. Rebecca lifted the skinny eight-year-old up the stairs. She immediately called her father to come home and take Jakie to the hospital. She reported that he tripped and fell down the stairs. Jakie's broken arm and leg were set and placed in a cast. Father was told it was Jakie's fault, because he was clowning around. The family knew differently.

After that episode, Jakie stood clear of Bertha and did as he was told. He knew when he reached eighteen he would enlist in the Army like Benny to escape his life of hell, especially after listening to Benny's exciting adventures describing his four years of service. Benny brought laughter to the household as he imitated his officers giving orders at boot camp and training for combat. However, with all his antics, Benny was suffering from severe headaches. He tried to treat them with cold compresses and medication, but they were more frequent and intense. Finally, Rebecca couldn't listen to Benny's complaints any longer and called Dr. Saperstein. She described the symptoms over the phone.

"Doctor, Benny's head is pounding. He is dizzy and sometimes has double vision. He breaks out in a sweat and shakes."

"Rush him to the hospital and I will meet you there within a half hour." After days of tests, Dr. Saperstein studied the results and conferred with other doctors.

They concluded that Benny had a brain tumor. Due to the location and the aggressiveness of the cancer, the tumor was inoperable.

When Benny came home and explained to Becky what the doctor told him, she tried to act brave for Benny's sake, but her emotions were fragile.

"I didn't think another member of our family would encounter cancer. I hate that word," she shouted with tears flowing down her checks.

"Shush," whispered Benny as he took his sister and cradled her in his arms. "I don't want anyone else to know until it gets bad. I want to be treated as a healthy man. I have medication for the pain, and that will get me through the rough times. Towards the end, Dr. Saperstein will put me in the hospital, so I'm not a burden to anyone."

Rebecca asked, "How much longer do we have together?" He placed his finger on her mouth indicating the questions were over. The time came fast and, within six months, Rebecca visited Cedars Hospital daily to watch her brother die. He lay in bed unconscious. His skull was swollen, so it looked like one head growing on top of another. She remembered the look of hollowness in his face, his stare no longer existing. Two days later, his breath subsided and his agony was gone. Rebecca had no more tears to shed. She kissed his hand and whispered, "Go in peace, my brother, and join mother at your place of rest."

During the Shiva, father sat in silence, not believing that another loved one had been taken from him. Bertha complained about all the people tramping in and dirtying the house. What she really hated was staying home all week. When people came over to visit, however, she howled, "God took another one of my precious children."

Euphoria described the climate of the country during the roaring twenties—high rollers, flappers, and good times. But the shadow of death loomed over the Hooberman household. Rebecca was alive, but felt choked off from the living. Doom and gloom spilled over on everyone. So when Louie Hooberman arrived home on a windy March afternoon in 1929 and announced the family was moving to Detroit, excitement filled the room. Papa was taking a job in the automobile industry. *This is my chance*, thought fifteen-year-old Rebecca. *I'll meet my prince charming who'll sweep me off my feet. I will marry young, and escape my life of servitude.* Bertha was not only excited because her sister lived there, but she believed: *At last I can leave here and have my own house. This place was built for another mistress and, in my opinion, the décor is tasteless. Now is my chance to have what I always dreamed of: A red brick colonial with black shutters and wraparound porch. Inside, I want red velvet drapes with velvet furniture, and crystal everywhere. My darling sister will see how well I did in marriage.*

However, that was Bertha's problem: big dreams, big price tags, and always money owed. Her specialty was hiding debts.

Louie worked extra hours to give Bertha what she demanded but he couldn't understand where the money went. She always needed and wanted more.

"How can I clothe and feed these kids on what you give me?"

"Bertha, I work overtime when I can and make a decent wage at the railroad. It's never enough." Louie walked away discouraged. *I hope my higher wages as foreman on the assembly line will finally satisfy her.*

The house sold within a month, but the move was postponed until the end of the school year. Rebecca was in charge of packing. Bertha was too busy looking for knickknacks and antiques to be bothered with such a task. She reasoned, *my stepdaughter is so excited about leaving Johnstown, let her do the heavy work.* Rebecca wrapped meticulously, making sure the glassware and dishes were placed separately in heavy newspapers and marked "fragile." Suddenly, after most items were packed, Rebecca became frantic. She went through drawers and bureaus looking for pictures of her mother to take with her and found none. She questioned Bertha,

"Why can't I find any pictures of my mother?"

Bertha gave a smirk and turned to walk away. Rebecca sprung around her and said accusingly, "I know you destroyed them."

"There is no room for two women in this household."

Rebecca went to her father explaining how she wanted one picture of her mother before leaving her past behind.

"I know of one picture still intact. It was placed on your mother's gravestone and that's where it will stay."

Rebecca was devastated. There was nothing she could do. *Not only must I leave this wonderful house that my mother loved and had built, but dad won't let me take any memorabilia with me. I can only bring my memories.*

The move to Detroit proved harder and longer then anyone expected. Finding a house was even more challenging. The Hooberman clan stayed with Bertha's widowed sister, Sarah Schwartz, in cramped surroundings. Mattresses lined the bedroom floor. Each child slept on one with no complaints. The children agreed not to show their unhappiness. After a week of looking for houses, Louie and Bertha came home all excited.

Louie explained to Sarah, "We found a two-flat in the Hastings area. It will be a perfect investment for us. We'll rent the downstairs and our family will live upstairs."

As her husband talked, Bertha never showed disappointment over not fulfilling her dream. *I will get my house someday. Right now, I must be patient.* One thing Bertha insisted on was new furniture for the whole house except the children's rooms. Her two boys, Sammy and Ritchie, shared one bedroom and Rebecca shared her room with Lilly and her half-sister Rona. Jakie took the musty attic. After one month of painting, cleaning, and unpacking, the Hoobermans settled in. Adjusting to their new life in Detroit meant getting acquainted with the neighborhood, shopping downtown, and meeting new people. Sarah helped with the transition.

However, the fabric of America changed five months after their move and the country went from boom to bust. The stock market crashed in those dark days of October causing the value of stocks listed on the New York Exchange to decline by a third or more. Panic followed as people watched their monies being gobbled up. Runs on banks caused closings, as depositors withdrew their savings. With bank failures and the stock market collapse, the country went into a depression. Rebecca heard her father say, "The crash was due to bad Federal Reserve policies." However, to the average person it meant unemployment, bread lines and soup kitchens. Mr. Hooberman was still working but for less money. His renter lacked the funds to pay and moved out. Times were dismal. He thought, *Could it get worse?*

The bottom was reached in March, 1933, when stocks had declined by more than eighty percent. Suicides doubled. Louie pushed his tool cart on the streets making keys and working as a locksmith. The auto industry no longer needed his service.

Finally, President Roosevelt implemented the "New Deal" and slowly America came out of its worst economic time in history. However, for a large portion of the population, it took many more years until they could breathe a sigh of relief. Rebecca took in sewing to contribute extra money. Bertha cut her spending, fearful they might lose the house. Radio was their form of entertainment. Family fun was listening to *The Jack Benny Show* or *George Burns and Gracie Allen*. The new game *Monopoly* was in demand, but there were no extra funds for frills. Thank goodness Aunt Sarah gave the game as a gift, as it kept the kids entertained for hours.

With all the uncertainty, some cheer came into the Hooberman and Schwartzes' lives. Rebecca was in the kitchen washing dinner dishes when she heard a knock at the back door. Sarah was out of breath, as she ran in shouting for Bertha.

"I'm here, Sarah. What's all the excitement?"

"It's my Rachel. She got engaged."

Both women embraced, spoke rapidly, and interrupted each other with questions.

"So when do I meet him?"

"You'll meet him soon. I'm going to have an engagement party for the family to meet Sam. They plan to get married within six months. They don't want to wait. Rachel and Sam want to start a family as soon as they are married. You can't blame them. My Rachel is getting old. She's already twenty-five. Almost an old maid, pu, pu," spit Sarah, an old Yiddish custom for warding off bad luck.

"Sarah, times are so bad; how can you afford a wedding?"

"I asked Rachel the same question: How can you afford a place of your own?"

"So, what did she say?"

"Apparently, Sam has a good job at Sanders Confectionary and saved a lot of money through the years. He's twelve years older then Rachel."

Bertha couldn't wait to meet Sam Slavkosky and show off her home. She decided to have a Friday night Sabbath dinner before the party to get acquainted. Sarah was fuming. She knew what her sister was up to. *She just wants to show off her cooking and fancy furniture to make me look simple and unimportant*, thought Sarah. Sarah didn't object, however, as she thought it was better to have Bertha on her side than endure her scorn.

Keeping the house and children spick-and-span was Rebecca's job, while Bertha cooked for the family gathering. Sarah, Rachel, and Sam arrived before sundown and Sam was introduced to the Hooberman family. As he commented on the delicious aroma that floated through the house, Bertha melted with pride and couldn't wait to start serving.

"Come, everyone; gather around the table for our first dinner with Sam." The food started coming. First, chopped liver, followed by a savory chicken noodle soup with carrots and stuffed dumplings called kreplach. The main course was roasted chicken and beef brisket with golden roasted potatoes. There was plenty of salad, vegetables, and challah bread. Red wine was an important accompaniment. Last was Bertha's special chocolate torte. Louie boasted, "Bertha, you are the best cook."

When she wanted to make an impression, Bertha outdid herself, but most of the time, cooking was Rebecca's responsibility. Tonight, everyone smacked their lips and savored every morsel. Louie sat proud, but wondered, *How much did this gala dinner set me back?*

The hustle and bustle of wedding plans energized the Hooberman and Schwartz families and took a detour from money doldrums. The big event took place on a cool evening in March, 1932. Bertha spent six months helping her sister and niece with decisions on invitations, flowers, food, and decorations. Sarah didn't want to spend as much money on items as Bertha did for lacy tablecloths and flower center pieces, but again, she didn't want to rile her sister and Sam said it was no problem.

Rebecca twirled around the room, as she looked in the mirror at her beautiful, borrowed, royal blue long silk dress. Her reflection showed a grown girl of eighteen, with a petite rounded body and warm smile. She hoped the Hooberman spell was broken.

"We're finally going to a party instead of a funeral," she remarked to her little sister, Rona.

The family arrived at the synagogue just in time for the ceremony to begin, as they were always running late with Bertha trying to look perfect in her long beige lace dress. After breaking the glass under the Chuppa, a marriage canopy representing the beginning of their home together, radiant Rachel in her full long white gown covered in lace and beads came walking up the aisle with her new husband, Sam. Everyone greeted them with "Mazel tov." As Rebecca proceeded to the social hall, where the party began with hors d'oeuvres and drinks, she noticed eyes gazing upon her from across the room. The glare, so strong, felt like a lighting rod searing through her body. The slender gentleman dressed in a seemingly expensive wide legged gray wool vested suit had the look of dancer Fred Astaire. His 5'10" frame seemed tall to her less-than-five-foot stature. He never gazed away as he started walking toward her. Rebecca's face flushed, but she gave him a little smile of acknowledgement. *Oh my goodness, he's coming over to speak to me. What should I do? What should I say?* Before Rebecca had time to think, Nathan introduced himself and asked her for a dance. They spent the evening dancing and talking as if they were the only two people in the room. However, they didn't go unnoticed. Bertha had her eyes on both of them all night and chuckled to herself. *He would be a good catch for Rebecca. He looks important and he's dressed like he has money. What an added asset he would be to our family,* smiled Bertha. *I'll have to look into this situation and see how I can make it work for all of us.*

CHAPTER 6

▼

NATHAN (ROMANIA TO DETROIT) 1913-1934

Nathan ran out of the bedroom, where he slept with his two older brothers in a three-room shack situated in a rural Jewish ghetto of Romania. *I hope Harry left me a pair of pants and shoes to attend school,* he thought. Clothing was sparse in the Abromowitz household and the brothers had to share their few garments. Ever since his father had left for America to find work, the burden to grow food on their small patch of land and reap a little pittance from the sales fell on the shoulders of the two elder boys. Nathan's older sister, Anna, looked after the two youngest girls. Mama washed and sewed clothes for others to earn extra money and didn't have time to supply her own children with garb. Cooking for six, with limited resources, was a challenge. Her staples included flour, oats, and cabbage. From them, she made bread, porridge, and stuffed, fried, or stewed cabbage.

When Nathan entered the main room used for sitting, cooking, and eating, he found some britches, a mended white shirt, and a pair of shoes, one size too small, neatly spread on the table. A piece of paper was used to plug up the hole in the right shoe. *I knew mama would make sure I go to school today*, he smiled.

At age eight, Nathan wanted to learn to read, write, and do arithmetic. His natural artistic talent was already evident in his drawings. Nathan ran out the front door heading for the two-room schoolhouse about a mile away. His brothers warned him to be on guard when leaving his surroundings.

"Bullies are waiting to attack Jews."

Anti-Semitism was rampant in Romania in the early 1900's. The gentiles laughed and enjoyed taunting the ghetto Jews whenever the opportunity was ripe. Nathan never left the ghetto, but this day was special. He was leaving to start school. Nathan's nightmare began as he approached the open field leading to the schoolhouse. Suddenly, he noticed something strange. The leaves on the bushes were moving with unusual vigor. He got scared and started to run. Four boys leaped out and pounced on him. They started to beat him up, calling him a dirty Jew. One boy started to tug on his pants, ripping them as they came down. He shouted:

"We want to see your cut-up penis. I hear the Jews do funny things to a boy's penis."

All four started to laugh. Nathan was taken by such surprise that fear took over and he started to pee. The boys laughed even louder. *How much more shame must I take?* Nathan thought, *I can't go to school where kids hate me so much.* For now, however, surviving this ordeal was the only thing on his mind. When the kids started to play with his privates, he started to cry. They mocked, "Maybe we should do a little more cutting to make his penis look uglier." Nathan was horrified and his eyes bulged like saucers. He tried squirming and screaming, but they held him down and covered his mouth. The brutes, bent over trying to control Nathan, didn't see the villager approach. When the boys heard the noise they turned around and saw a man with a walking stick. They got up to run away, but before they left, the tall, bulky one whispered,

"If we catch you again, Jew boy, we'll hack off your ugly prick."

The old man, concerned when he saw Nathan on the ground, just imagined what the older boys were up to. Nathan got up and ran home as fast as his legs could take him. His days of attending school were over. He told his mother, "I don't like school. I'd rather stay home and help you."

When she found his torn clothes, she understood. Devorah learned that her son suffered humiliation that day, but didn't want to know the details. Extra trouble was not needed; surviving was the important task. Nathan resented his father for not being here to protect him. In fact, he could hardly remember his father at all. Periodically, a letter came from America saying:

"I'm working hard to save money for the family's passage to a free country. Love, Benny."

A year later, Benny sent enough money for his elder sons to come to America to work and vowed to send more for the rest. Now, Nathan resented his father even more. Not only was *he* gone, but he was taking away his brothers. At age nine, Nathan was considered the man of the house and had to help his mother grow vegetables, milk their one cow, and feed a few chickens. He would still not leave the ghetto. One year later, the money came for the rest of the family to leave their wretched life and sail to America.

It was a month at sea and many people lay in the bowels of the ship moaning and vomiting from the turbulence. Nathan kept away from the sick. He spent his time on deck drawing and dreaming of his new life in America. He imagined walking the streets without getting beaten up. He heard that if one worked hard, one could make lots of money in this new place. As the tale goes, "the streets are paved with gold."

The family entered the United States through Canada. They crossed the border at Windsor and came by trolley to Detroit. The trip was long and exhausting, but no one complained. *Finally, the family will be together*, thought Devorah. She hadn't seen her husband in four years. *Would he still find me attractive? Did this new country change him?* She secretly pondered these questions and was afraid of the answers. As the family got off the trolley, Nathan recognized his brothers right away. He waved and shouted "Over here! We're over here!"

Everyone greeted each other with hugs and kisses. Benny took his wife in his arms and whispered, "Oh how I missed you, Devorah."

She knew everything was going to be all right.

The best part of America for Nathan was attending school, even if it was for a short time. He learned English without much difficulty, but math and writing were a bit harder. Nathan never got the opportunity to go to art school. By the time he was fourteen, he had to quit school to work laboriously with his father peddling fruits and vegetables on the streets of Detroit. Every morning they rose at 4:30 a.m. to go to the wholesalers and buy fresh produce. They piled the merchandise on the wagon and were ready to sell their wares by 6:00. *Thank goodness mama was up making grits before we left or I would be starving*, thought Nathan. Papa wouldn't stop to eat the lunch Devorah packed until most of his items were sold. Nathan didn't find his pot of gold like in his dream; just a lot of hard work in a country demanding change.

Harold, the eldest son, found work in the auto factory, but not before changing his name from Abromowitz to Abrom, so people wouldn't know he was Jewish. Henry Ford would never hire a Jew. His other brother, Lawrence, used the name Abrom to get a job at Sanders.

Nathan was getting restless. He was tired of schlepping produce and wasn't getting paid much by his father. By the time he was eighteen, he knew he needed a good job, but what? Meanwhile, Lawrence was promoted. Instead of baker, he was in charge of cake decorating and made $30 a week.

"Nathan, come join me at Sanders. There is a job opening for a beginner baker with opportunities to advance."

"I don't know anything about baking," he replied.

"You don't need to know. You'll start as an apprentice. You've got talent with your hands. Look at all those beautiful drawings you do. You can learn to decorate cakes just as beautifully."

Nathan thought over what Lawrence said and realized he would never attend drawing school, because he needed money. "When do I start?"

Nathan applied the next day and used Abrom as his last name. Since he was Lawrence's brother, he got the job and started immediately. Telling his father wasn't easy, but he knew he had to change the direction of his life. He did his job well, advanced rapidly, and worked throughout the Depression. Nathan and his brothers contributed money to the household and still had extra to save. His friend and co-worker Sam explained:

"You should buy bonds. That's how you get ahead in this country."

Nathan took his money that he had hidden in the house and bought U.S. Savings Bonds. He started to feel like a real American. Dressing nicely was important, as the days of sharing clothes with his brothers in Romania were still etched in his mind. Saving to buy a car with Lawrence also meant status.

Possessions, however, weren't enough. He was lonely and needed to find someone to share his life. It was time to leave his parents' home. When Sam announced that he was getting married, he invited Nathan to the wedding. At first, he was hesitant and joked, "I won't know anyone there but you Sam and I think you'll be rather occupied."

"You'll meet people. Come at least to the ceremony and have dinner. If you feel uncomfortable then leave, but I want you to meet my Rachel."

Finally, Nathan agreed. The wedding took place at the Hasting Street Synagogue. Nathan watched all the people enter and felt a little apprehensive as he approached the front door. He couldn't turn back now and disappoint his friend. He made it through the ceremony and stood around eating hors d'oeuvres, when his eyes affixed on the most beautiful round face staring back at him. He thought his heart would stop, but instead it started beating faster and faster. *I must meet this girl with a complexion like a fresh peach not yet ripened and dimples that make her face light up every time she smiles.* As he approached her, he hoped to find the right words to say. He thought about first asking for a dance to relieve the tension. Thank goodness, his sister, Dorothy, had taught him how to waltz. After the dance, they sat and talked most of the evening. He told her that he knew Sam from work and about his dream of being an artist.

"I'll show you my drawings."

"I'd love to see them."

She told him of her mundane life at home and how she hoped to find work at an office or shop, and save money to buy beautiful clothes.

After the wedding, Nathan walked Rebecca home. He asked her if he could see her again and she agreed. They courted for six months. Nathan knew she was the one, but Rebecca wasn't sure if he was "Mr. Right." There was a ten-year age difference between them and she thought he was too old for her, since she was only eighteen. Bertha was excited about Rebecca meeting such a handsome man with a secure job, a rarity for the times.

"Look at the car he drives, Rebecca. It's that new LaSalle by Cadillac that everyone's talking about. He could give you all the luxuries you want. Don't hesitate; he's a good catch."

Bertha thought, *maybe there will be a little extra money for me.* Rebecca was confused and didn't know what to do. Nathan couldn't wait any longer and proposed. Rebecca was honest with him.

"I don't know if I really love you or if I would be marrying you just to get out of the house."

"I love you with all my heart and in time you will learn to love me. You are my little Becky and our life together will be good. I will do anything for you."

She still had doubts, but thought about her destiny in the Hooberman household and consented. Like the poem in her diary, Nathan was the rescuer.

After her acceptance, Becky went to meet the Abromowitz family and set the date for the wedding. Nate (Becky's nick-name for him) had filled her in on so many stories about the family's arrival to America. Bertha called them "Romanian Greenies." Becky couldn't understand why. Bertha, like her own family, came from Russia with similar experiences.

Bertha invited Benny and Devorah Abromowitz over for Sabbath dinner so the families could get acquainted. Bertha was dressed in a printed ankle-length yellow silk dress and Devorah wore black with a white collar. Devorah found all the velvet and crystal in Bertha's home garish, as she thought about her used wool couch and chair with worn shiny spots. Bertha talked about making a big wedding and the Abromowitzs said nothing. Becky saw the overwhelmed look on Benny and Devorah's faces and knew she had to step in. She knew her father didn't have the money to pay for a large wedding and Bertha would be asking Nate to pay. She grabbed Nate's hand and they both stood up.

"We decided to have a ceremony in the Rabbi's chamber with only family and a few close friends. A dinner will follow afterwards."

Nate was relieved to hear those words and squeezed her hand to acknowledge his approval. His parents sat quietly, but a faint smile came across their faces and Becky and Nate knew they made the right decision. Bertha sat down in a huff, but knew she was defeated.

Lilly felt all grown up when her big sister asked her to come along and help select a wedding dress. Becky didn't want Bertha's two cents in any decision and didn't want to go alone. Nate gave her enough money to buy the most exquisite gown and knew Bertha would select the most expensive. Becky didn't want to abuse his generosity. When the girls entered Ray's Bridal Salon on Woodward Avenue, their mouths fell open to see such elegance. Lilly whispered, "I never thought I'd be in a place like this."

"Me neither."

The saleslady, with a bun piled on top of her silver gray hair, approached the girls.

"I'm Miss Charlotte. Which one is the lucky bride-to-be?"

Lilly wished she could say it was her, as she dreamt so many times about a special person like Nathan scooping her away to a fairyland like in *Peter Pan*. Becky beamed with joy as she explained to Miss Charlotte the type of dress she pictured in her mind.

"I want a white satin long gown, with no train, puffy sleeves, and stand-up collar."

"I think I can find the perfect dress for you."

Becky and Lilly giggled with excitement, while waiting for Charlotte to return. The first dress she brought in had a bouffant skirt and Becky pictured her short frame looking like an apple. Than came the next and the next. Becky felt discouraged. As she put on her clothes and started to leave, Charlotte came rushing in holding the most beautiful ivory long satin gown with a v-neckline. The dress was sleeveless, but had a brown satin jacket with puffy sleeves and stand-up collar exactly as Becky had described it.

"This was just unpacked and I thought it would be perfect for you."

She gently assisted Becky with stepping into the dress. The moment she saw her image in the mirror, Becky knew this was the one. The slender silhouette flattered her torso and a sleeveless gown would be perfect for August. Becky loved the lines of the jacket and knew it was just right. Lilly marveled at how beautiful her sister looked and pictured herself one day in a special bridal gown. The seamstress was called to pin the hem. Becky was told it would be ready in two weeks. "Perfect," she said, and proceeded to get dressed.

Miss Charlotte asked, "What about veiling?"

"I want to stop at Greta's Millinery Shop to look for an ivory satin hat to wear instead of a veil, but thank you."

"Lilly, I love coming to Greta's shop," said Becky, as she opened the door. "I look for any excuse to visit."

Lilly coaxed, "Why don't you ask for a job? This is your chance to do something for yourself now that you'll be out of Bertha's domain." *How wise my sister is for being only fourteen,* Becky thought. "Oh, I don't know. I'll ask Nate if he would mind if I worked outside the house."

"Well, at least talk with Greta to see if she would hire you. I don't think Nate would object to anything you wanted to do."

They laughed. Becky shook her head in agreement and started looking for that special ivory cap. Becky tried to stay calm as she placed her bridal garments on the bed. August 14, 1932, was her day to become Mrs. Abrom. *I can't believe my wedding day arrived so quickly. I hope I'm doing the right thing,* thought Becky, as she nervously started dressing. Lilly knocked on the door to see if she could help.

"I've got the wedding jitters, but I'm all right."

Even Bertha appeared in the doorway to see if she could help. Lilly and Becky looked at each other in disbelief.

When the Hoobermans arrived at the synagogue, Nathan and family were already waiting. They entered the Rabbi's chambers and stood watching for Becky to make her entrance.

As the doors opened, Becky started walking towards Nathan. He couldn't take his eyes off his beautiful bride. Becky admired Nate. How smashing he looked in his black tuxedo. She started to feel at ease. *I am making the right choice, she thought.* They stood together, under the Chuppa, repeating the words from the Rabbi. To seal the marriage in the Jewish tradition, Nate stepped on the glass and passionately kissed his wife.

The small dinner in the social hall with family and friends finalized the celebration. Devorah sat quietly at the table watching Bertha give orders to the staff on the proper way to serve. *I only hope Bertha doesn't interfere with Becky and Nate's life,* she worried.

CHAPTER 7

▼

MARRIAGE WITH BABY

After the wedding, the couple spent a week at Niagara Falls and returned to their cozy little two-bedroom apartment near Clairmount and Owen. Becky hopped on the Clairmount streetcar to start her new job at Greta's Millinery shop, as a saleslady. When she entered the hat shop, Becky felt she was in her own magical world. She imagined that each hat told a story. After she put on a beige felt hat with an orange feather jetting out on her head, she closed her eyes and pictured a high society lady in a beige suit, with a long skirt, walking her small poodle along the fir-treed boulevard, while greeting influential people. Changing to a small black sequined hat, she pictured a woman in a short black shimmy dress entering a speakeasy with her beau by her side. As Becky opened her eyes and gently placed the hat on its stand, a customer entered and inquired about a hat appropriate for lunches and going to church. Becky retrieved the beige felt one with the orange feather.

"I have just the one for you," she smiled.

Riding the streetcar to her job gave Becky a feeling of freedom. No more whining voices, runny noses, and bad behavior from her half-siblings. She still helped out on weekends, however, because Bertha complained about all the hard work and Becky thought it was her duty to give assistance; but lately, she felt extremely tired.

Heavy rain beat against the windows and pavement and sent chills through Becky's body as she thought about leaving for work. *I hate going out in this damp May weather.* She felt nauseous and weak, but continued dressing and then ran to the toilet to vomit. *I wonder, what's the matter with me? I can't even make it to the bus stop.* She called Greta to explain what was happening to her. Greta understood and told her to stay home, but to herself wondered if Becky was pregnant.

"Promise me one thing, Becky; if you don't start feeling better you'll go see your doctor."

Becky agreed and then went to lie down. When the symptoms continued every morning for two weeks, Becky made an appointment with Dr. Kline.

"Did you miss any periods, Becky?"

"I'm not always regular, but I think it was two."

"Lie down and let me examine you."

After the examination, Dr. Kline said, "Congratulations. Becky, you're going to be a mother."

Becky was excited and couldn't wait to get home and tell Nate. *How should I break the news to him?* She never told him about her morning sickness. *I know he loves children and becoming a father will make him the happiest man.*

Becky stopped at the corner meat market and bought veal chops to make Nate his favorite meal. They dined by candle-light for the right atmosphere; and when Becky said she had an announcement to make, Nate thought she received a raise or was promoted to manager. When she broke the news, Nate was stunned.

"I can't believe we're going to have a baby." He gave her a hug and twirled her around. "My child will be born in America and never have to endure the hardships that my family and I had in the old country."

Nathan choked and made Becky teary-eyed. After four months, Becky started to feel better. She worked until her sixth month and then quit to prepare for the baby's arrival.

The blanket of snow sparkled from the sun's rays sending a false sense of warmth on a bitter cold January 17, 1934. Becky's water broke and Nate got the signal they needed to leave for the hospital. The intensity and frequency of the contractions increased and Nate knew he better hurry. However, the nip in the air made the snow icy and driving fast wasn't an option.

"Hold on, Beck; we're almost there."

Becky controlled the screams that were trying to come out, because she didn't want to scare Nate. Finally, they arrived and Becky was taken to the examining room to determine how far she was dilating. Nate was told to go to the waiting room, while

Becky was prepared for delivery. Five hours went by and Nate became worried. He paced the floor. *Something must have gone wrong.* His fear increased. *Why doesn't someone come out and tell me what's happening?* Fear took over Becky as her pain increased. However, as soon as ether was given, she couldn't remember anything about the birth. Finally, after six hours, the doctor came out to discuss the delivery.

"Nathan, your wife and little girl are fine, but don't get upset over the shape of the baby's head. I had to use instruments to force her out of the womb. Probably by the time they leave, the baby's head will return to being round."

The first time the nurse brought the baby to Becky, she was taken aback by her pear-shaped head. Dr. Kline explained to Becky that it would change within a week. She was concerned, but afraid to say anything to Nate. He was so enthralled with his daughter that he saw only beauty. As they watched their creation, Becky inquired if they could name the baby after her mother, Reva. They compromised on Rena. After two weeks in the maternity ward, she was ready to take her precious bundle home. Upon entering the car, Nate and Becky took a few minutes to sit in contentment. They smiled and confirmed how lucky they were to be a family. Then they heard small gurgles under the blanket and started to laugh. Becky made an opening in the cloth to admire beautiful Rena. Her little head changed to the shape of a round plum.

CHAPTER 8

▼

MEMORIES

Becky tossed and turned in bed. She felt restless on the evening before her discharge. *I can't believe I'm leaving tomorrow after one year in this hospital.* Becky was anxious to get out, but fearful of the future. *My daughter no longer knows me and cries at my sight. I'm limping and wearing a brace. I feel like an invalid. I remember my shapely legs.* She laughed, *Nate use to call them the "Betty Grable" legs. Now, one leg is scarred for life. I keep telling myself, be thankful you're alive. But my tears won't stop.*

Becky recalled the night they brought her into the hospital. The burning, piercing pain was too much to bear, as she fell unconscious and remained so for a few days. As time passed so did the surgeries. One day she lay in bed bored and started counting: *They repaired my internal injuries, crushed leg, and removed the tumor that formed from the leg cast rubbing against my outer thigh. Morphine shots were the magic bullet that reduced the agony. Thank goodness for Lilly, my wonderful sister who came to visit daily and kept me laughing when I wanted to scream out, "Why me?"*

Then tears started trickling down her cheek, as Becky thought about the visit her father-in-law paid about a month after the accident.

"Beckala, if you didn't run around so much, maybe this wouldn't have happened."

Can you imagine? He blamed me for this whole mess. "I'm just the victim," she wept.

My beloved, Nate. What would I do without you? I remember the words you said on the night you proposed: "You will learn to love me." My love for you has grown through this past year. Instead of running scared, you stuck by me and took on two jobs to pay the bills.

While in bed, she continued to reminisce. *With the bitterness comes sweetness,* as she recalled her early years when life was not so cruel. *Mother used to tell me the story of how Grandpa Shlomo held me in his arms, as the family boarded the ship leaving Russia in 1917 for the free world. We were escaping the Russian pogroms designed to terrorize the Jews. As a one-year-old, I didn't understand persecution, but when I saw terror in mother's eyes, it frightened me.*

Mama said the passengers aboard the ship pinched my rosy cheeks and talked to me, but I didn't understand. One day with my curls still wet from washing, grandpa took me on the upper deck. The strong wind whipped around the galley. It grabbed my ear with a vengeance and gave me an earache. Medication was limited and by the time I saw a doctor, the ear was infected. My ear still drains at times and gives me problems and there are no medical answers.

Funny, reasoned Becky, *my family saved money and took chances to get visas to escape and protect me from suffering. However, since the age of twelve, I have endured heartache.* Still, Becky smiled. *I remember the big house in Johnstown and the train trips with my mother to visit relatives in Pittsburgh and Cleveland. Father, a conductor on the Pennsylvania Railroad, never had a problem getting tickets. Mommy, how I miss you. Your petite figure concealed a big heart. You were so giving, always cooking and baking for the needy or taking food over to someone sick at home. Daddy was robust in size, but quiet in demeanor. He left the household matters to you. He never played much with me like Nate plays with Rena, but I believed he cared.* Becky dreamt about the day she turned age ten. *It was a special birthday and mom was going to have my friends over for cake and ice cream. As the party was ending, papa came over with a little box to reveal a beautiful cameo pendant.*

"Oh papa, it's so lovely. I will always keep it close to me."

She walked around with pride, the necklace dangling from her neck. *I'll never forget the day I nearly lost my treasure and thought I could never face my father again.*

Becky's fingers touched the cameo, as if electrifying impulses jogged her memory. *I was swinging the sculpted figure up and down my chain at school trying to calm my nerves over Miss Schultz's math test. When classes ended, I met my friend, Jean, to start our journey home. Sometimes we walked, ran, or played hopscotch following the same path. I didn't feel the pendant slip away from my body.*

After saying goodbye to Jean, I ran inside the house and hung up my coat. I reached to touch my necklace, but my neck was bare. I couldn't believe it. What happened to my cameo? I ran outside to catch up with my friend, crying hysterically.

"It's lost, it's lost."

"What are you talking about?"

"My cameo necklace is not around my neck. It must have fallen off as we were coming home. What am I going to do?"

"Calm down. We'll backtrack our route home and look for the necklace."

The two girls walked hand in hand looking carefully on the ground scouting for a tiny lady silhouette framed in gold. They walked back to the school and found nothing. Rebecca's face hung low and her eyes swelled with tears.

"Don't cry again. I can't stand listening to the sobs. We'll find it."

"No, we won't. My father never gave me my own personal gift before. I'll never forgive myself if I can't find it."

"I've got an idea. Let's walk slowly and bend down to look for it closer to the ground."

They both started slowly down the path again, carefully watching each step. They noticed some older girls walking towards them. A tall lanky girl with a short bob haircut approached,

"What are you two doing on the ground? Is everything all right?"

Rebecca couldn't hold back the tears any longer and started to tell her saga. The girl, whose name was Joyce, looked over to her friend Molly.

"Remember the pendant you found on the ground? I think it belongs to her."

"How do you know? Let her describe it."

Rebecca controlled her tears long enough to give an exact description of the necklace. Satisfied, Molly handed the cameo over to her.

"It didn't have a chain and the gold rim is bent."

"Oh, thank you so much. I'll get it fixed. It means so much to me."

Rebecca never got it fixed until she married Nathan. She never had the money for repairs. She couldn't ask her father. He wasn't to know what happened. However, it didn't matter. He never noticed Rebecca wasn't wearing it. His mind was preoccupied with keeping his wife alive. After her death, his time was consumed with finding a replacement to keep the family continuity. Becky's bitterness was erupting, as her memories unfolded.

I need to stay focused, she told herself. *I can't let the devastation consume my life. My little girl was left for a whole year without her mother just like I was left without my mother.* She started to whimper. *Rena wakes up in a different home with different people. Friends and relatives are caring for her, but to be left with Bertha, of all people! I barely escaped her abuse. How did she treat my poor daughter? Tomorrow I will have my baby back. My life changed drastically in one year, but I need to make it work. No matter how much pain, I will go on.*

Becky thought about the day the doctor took off her cast and told her the physical therapist would teach her to walk again. The leg felt heavy and numb. *How was I to move it, let alone stand and walk?* Jenny, the therapist, was patient. *With every scream, I took a step and she was there with encouragement. Now I limp, but I can walk. Jenny says that in time I won't need a brace and will increase my distance.*

Finally, morning arrived and Becky was out of bed and dressed waiting for Nate to pick her up. Her big day: she was going home to join her family.

CHAPTER 9

▼

GOING HOME

Nate had an extremely hard and demanding work schedule. *After four hours of sleep, I'm on the bus going to my second job. My supervisor at Sanders doesn't know I work in a small pastry shop in Hamtramck. I was lucky the owner needed a baker to relieve him from noon to 5:00 p.m. My job was baking rolls, cakes, and pastries on the second work shift. Then, it's off to see Rena for an hour. How I miss spending time with her. I know she doesn't understand what's happening because she cries every time I leave her. No mother and a brief visit from her father. What can I do? I need to go to the hospital and see my dear Becky.*

The bills are piling up. I sold my car, the bonds, and used the savings. I can't believe I'm as poor as when I came from Romania. Who can I go to for help? No one, he answered. *Once Becky comes home from the hospital and I'm not running to babysitters, I can find a third job. I can function without much rest.*

It happened on the balmy first day of spring in 1936. Nate arrived at Receiving Hospital with his brother, Lawrence, at 10:00 a.m. check-out time. Today, happiness would pour back into Nate's life. He was bringing home his wife and child. Before departing, the head nurse gave Nate a list of do's and dont's that Becky needed to follow at home to allow her body to mend.

"Let's go, Nate. I can't wait to see Rena."

Lawrence went to get the car and Nate went to the cashier to settle the bill. He was short twenty-five cents. "We can't release her until the bill is paid in full," complained the girl behind the cage. Nate ran out to get change from his brother. After a signed release, Becky was wheeled to the exit door. Before leaving, she hugged and said goodbye to everyone that participated in her care. Nate brought Sanders' candy for the nurses on every shift. He collected the accumulated articles, placed them in a wheel-chair, and followed out the door. Becky's last words on her way out: "You won't see me here again."

The last stop was Bertha's house to pick up Rena. Rena saw her father come in the house and she ran to him with glee.

"Daddy, daddy, I want to go home."

"That's where we're going pumpkin, and I have a surprise for you."

Rena was all excited. She loved surprises, but when she got to the car and saw that strange woman sitting there, she started to cry. Bertha was right behind them.

"What do you expect? She hasn't seen her for a year. We're more her family than Becky. I hope you can get back to taking care of your home and child, because I'm tired from everything that was expected of me."

Bertha turned around and walked into her house without looking back.

Now Nate's routine had an added dimension. He helped Becky with grocery shopping, cleaning, and caring for Rena. Becky's standing tolerance on her leg was limited and too much stress could put her back into the hospital. Nate handled her with kid gloves and no one ever heard him complain of his multi-tasks and double work load.

CHAPTER 10

▼

RENA (1935-1936)

Since her mother's disappearance six months ago, Rena felt bewildered, frightened, and lonely. At a year and a half, Rena couldn't grasp the reason her mother no longer was at home caring for her. She began to act out her frustration by whining, crying, eating less, and sleeping more. Rena saw her father for an hour on days he dropped her off at different relatives' homes. Sometimes when she slept over at their house, she didn't see him at all. At some places, there were other children so she received a lot of attention and played with their toys. However, the worst was with grandmother Bertha, her "Bubbie."

"Don't touch anything. It's all crystal and glass that can break. Go sit in the corner of the kitchen and if you move, I'll slap you."

Rena tried walking into other rooms, but was slapped on the legs and brought back to the kitchen. Finally, she stayed in a corner of the floor with her blanket and thumb in her mouth until she fell asleep. The next day, the same routine was repeated.

A week later, Nate came to pick up Rena to take her to a place she had never seen before. Rena looked bewildered at the big building that contained so many people. She wondered, *Who was that lady sitting in a funny chair with big wheels and the other lady dressed in white pushing her around? Why does the lady in the chair have white paper wrapped around her leg?* Becky grabbed her child and gave a big hug and kissed her on the check. Rena didn't understand.

"I'm your mother."

Rena moved her head away and cried.

It took a year before the Abrom family was united. Becky came home from the hospital with a brace on her leg and a list of limitations. She was not to abuse her leg, so kneeling on her knees to wash floors was out. Gaining weight was not advised, as her leg could not support an excess load. That meant no more pregnancies.

Rena looked surprised to see the lady with the funny metal on her leg come into their house to stay. Nate assured her, "This is your mother."

"I don't want her here, daddy. You go away."

Rena heard her daddy command, "Call her mother, Rena. She belongs here with us."

Since Becky returned home, life became stable for Rena. She had her own surroundings, played with her toys, and spent more time with her father. One thing she learned about the new lady called mother. Becky had a whole new set of rules to follow.

CHAPTER 11

▼

THE ADJUSTMENT

Time was friend and foe to Becky. She used it to gain strength and endurance. Her walking improved and within a year she was able to discard her brace. However, Rena's behavior was the problem and time didn't change it. Age two was the defiant year. She said "No" to everything. If Becky told her not to touch the walls with dirty hands, she did it anyway. Rena's diaper was her companion for two more years. She cried at night for her father, but he was at work. Becky was in no shape to deal with a hysterical child.

Becky's dreams were getting worse. She woke up with sweat at the nape of her neck, down her face, and under her breastbone. Her breathing was heavy and she wanted to scream out, but covered her mouth so Rena wouldn't hear. *My leg! Where is my leg?* Becky felt nothing of her right leg. The feeling was that a knife had sliced it off. She reached down; her leg was intact.

Why does it burn so badly and feel like sharp pins stuck into a voodoo doll? She got up, wiped her tears, and went to stop Rena's crying. She coddled the child, gave her some milk, and put her back to bed. Sometimes Becky's pain took over her patience and she left Rena to cry herself back to sleep.

When Nate came home in the morning, Becky cried, "What happened to my jovial baby, who used to giggle and wear a smile on her face? I swear Rena must be punishing me for abandoning her. I couldn't help it. How do you tell a youngster it wasn't your fault? When are my awful dreams going to end? My head hurts from lack of sleep."

"Becky, maybe you should see a doctor and find out what's wrong," Nate said.

He was concerned over his daughter and wife's behavior, but didn't know how to handle it. If she started with doctors, it meant more bills and he couldn't handle more than three jobs. They had finally started to come out of debt. Luckily, he found a job at the butcher shop near their apartment. He came home from Sanders, grabbed something to eat and went to cut chops and chickens until the afternoon. He came home, played a game with Rena, slept a few hours, and left for his second job. When he came back from the pastry shop, he had just enough time to eat and go to sleep before leaving for Sanders. No matter how tired, when home, Nate was available to listen to Becky's problems.

"Nate, I find this apartment suffocating. It's too small to maneuver with a crib, high chair, and toys all over. We need a bigger place. I know we don't have much money saved, but we can rent a larger flat."

"Okay, honey. I'm making enough that we can afford a higher rent. You go look at some places and when you find what you like, I'll take a look before working at Hymie's Meat Market."

Becky gave Nate a hug and went to call Lilly to see if she wanted to join her and Rena to look at flats.

"Where should we go to look, Lilly? It's hard to leave the Hastings area. I feel safe in my surroundings with the hustle and bustle of the Jewish community."

Shops, restaurants and businesses catered to her cultural needs. Synagogues lined the corridor of Hastings and Becky wanted to join the sisterhood of B'nai Olm. She remembered trying to find housing further North, but was confronted with signs that read "No Negroes—No Jews—No Dogs."

She recalled Millie telling her a new area was becoming popular among her friends at the Linwood and Dexter corridor. Three schools lined together on Burlingame and Linwood beginning with Elementary and finishing with High School. It was predominately a gentile area, but more and more Jews were moving in and Jewish merchants followed. Becky got the paper out and circled the places to visit. They'd travel by bus since cab fare was too expensive and no one had a car. She told everyone that Nate sold his car because of her fear of automobiles since the accident. The truth was they needed money to pay bills and couldn't afford the price tag or expense of a car. The three of them combed the area with disappointment. The flats were too small, too dirty or too expensive.

"Another discouraging day," sighed Lilly.

"Thanks for going with me. I don't know what I would do without you."

Lilly was hesitant about going on with the conversation, but knew she had to tell Becky of her decision.

"I don't know how to tell you this Becky, so I'm just going to say it."

"What is it, Lilly?"

"I'm moving to Chicago and looking for a job at one of their department stores."

"Don't go. Find a job here at Hudson's or Kern's."

"No, Becky. I've got to get out of the house and far away. I'll miss you and your family, but I need a new beginning."

"I'll miss you so much."

Becky hugged Lilly and choked back the tears. "When are you leaving?"

"In about two weeks. Don't worry, I'll be back to visit. Chicago isn't that far away and I'll write every week."

Becky was walking around gloomily thinking about how much she missed her sister, when Nate came home from Hymie's all excited.

"Becky, one of my customers told me about a four-flat on a street called Monterey. It's off Linwood not too far from the Roosevelt Elementary School. In another couple of years, we'll have to think about Rena starting kindergarten. Let's go look tomorrow. Hymie said I can come in a little late for work."

Right after Nate came home from Sanders, the Abroms hopped on the Linwood bus and ventured to a new area. They walked one block from the bus stop and three doors from the corner of Lawton Street; they approached an immaculate red brick four-family residence with flawless bent grass and manicured bushes. Each flat had its own porch. The downstairs flat was as immaculate as the outside. Becky fell in love with it. The kitchen was small and had only space for two people to eat, but Nate was never home long enough to eat with the family. If they had a holiday dinner, there was a large dining room.

The landlord and his daughter lived above them and another daughter and her family lived in the other upper flat. Beneath them and across the hall from the Abroms' flat lived an older widow, who kept to herself.

"This place is perfect," shouted Becky with joy.

Nate hadn't seen her this happy for so long. It was refreshing. "Shall we take it, Beck?"

"Of course, but can we afford it?"

"I think we can swing it," smiled Nate.

Becky couldn't wait to write Lilly and tell her all about the new place she was moving to within a month. However, that night the phone rang and it was Lilly with news of her own.

"Lilly, I'm so glad you called. I just wrote you a letter telling you about our good news."

"I also have good news."

"Tell me your news first," commanded Becky.

"Well, I met this most wonderful man and we've been dating for a couple of weeks. If we become serious and he proposes, we'll move back to Detroit.

"Who is your dreamboat, Lilly?"

"Stephen Collins. He is a salesman for a woman's clothing line and his company wants him to open the Detroit market."

"How much do you know about him?"

"Be happy for me Becky and stop acting like a big sister. I know he's handsome and charming and I'm in love. Now tell me about your news."

"We found a new place to live. It's in an up-and-coming Jewish area, but not as popular as Hastings and the Clairmount vicinity. So prices are not as high. We share the building with three other families, but they seem nice and the landlord lives upstairs and keeps the place impeccable."

"It sounds great. When are you moving?"

"Our lease is up in three weeks, so we'll probably move within a month. I'm busy going through items and packing."

"Did you ask the witch to help?"

"Are you kidding? Our relationship is totally strained. Today, she's not talking to me, because I don't come around and help her clean. She reminds me of all the work she did caring for Rena when I was in the hospital."

"Some things never change. So how is Rena?"

"She's still withdrawn and plays alone in her bedroom until Nate comes home and plays a quick game with her. At least now she listens and doesn't have so many tantrums, but I still think she's angry with me."

"You don't know that for sure."

"No, I feel her resentment or it's my own guilt that makes me feel it. Lilly, if you do marry and come back to Detroit, maybe you can find a place near us. It will be like old times."

"Don't get too excited Becky. It's way too early to know, but I'll keep you informed. Give everyone my love."

It was moving day and Nate took off from his two jobs to help. The blistery hot summer took its toll on Becky as she worked harder than her doctors would approve. Her body ached, her leg throbbed, and she was sweaty. The job needed to get done and Becky became obsessed with how she wanted her flat to look. Nate promised that they could buy new living room furniture and save for a dining room set. They used the bedroom furniture from the apartment. It was a beautiful mahogany shaded wood dresser, which had a vanity, a round mirror, and bench to match. The double bed rested on a frame with head and foot boards. This room of furniture was their first purchase after the wedding when money wasn't an issue. *How time has changed our financial picture*, Becky thought, as the movers placed the bedroom set where she directed. Becky borrowed a junior bed from a friend for Rena, as she was too big for the crib.

"Someday we'll get you a new set, Rena. Right now this will have to do."

Rena didn't care. She just wanted to play with her dolls and toys. Once settled, Becky's mission was getting out and meeting neighbors. She wanted to find friends for her daughter, but

Rena kept to herself. "I know this place will change our lives for the better," she said.

However, the future change was not what Becky expected. A year passed before Becky was acclimated to her new surroundings. The people living upstairs took in the Abroms like family. They exchanged special treats. The Wilburs sent down Christmas cookies and cakes during the holiday. At Easter, they gave Rena a basket full of chocolates and jelly beans. Becky sent up special food for Passover for everyone to taste. They gave Becky a hand with shopping or running errands, so Becky preserved her energy. Even Rena enjoyed assisting the Wilbur family with decorating the Christmas tree, making cookies or sledding with the older Wilbur children.

During this time, Becky recognized a transformation taking place. The neighborhood was changing from gentile to Jewish. Shop owners were moving from the old neighborhood to Dexter and Linwood. Grocery, bakery, and butcher shops couldn't open fast enough. Kosher delicatessens and other restaurants were in demand. Synagogues sprouted in every direction. Becky's support system was in place. Friends were established in a closely knitted community.

CHAPTER 12

▼

RAYMOND MILLER, JR. (1935-1936)

The chugging rhythm of the train from Detroit to New York made Raymond feel anxious and become fidgety. He kept to himself while fuming because his father had sent him away. He knew it was to protect him from any investigation concerning the accident, but he couldn't stop wallowing in self-pity. *I know I have to get my life together, but my father is more concerned with his career than with me.* Suddenly, his thoughts were interrupted when he heard the conductor yell, "Last stop! New York Grand Central."

As he disembarked the train and made his way out of the building, he saw a driver in a uniform waving a sign with his name on it. *This must be the person my father hired to drive me to the clinic. He doesn't miss a trick,* chuckled Raymond. *He's probably afraid I'd take off and hide out somewhere in Manhattan.*

That's not a bad idea. Something to think about if this place stifles me. Raymond took a deep breath and started towards the driver.

Mr. Potts inquired, "Are you Master Miller?" He grabbed the young man's bags without waiting for an answer.

Once out of Manhattan, the ride to Riverdale calmed Raymond. The scenery changed from a busy city to hilly terrain surrounded by virgin land. He smelled freshness in the air that made him forget his troubles. *I feel like a newborn starting from the beginning. I smell great opportunities here.* Suddenly, the car took a turn onto a dirt road. His eyes abruptly opened, taking him out of his dreamy state. After a short distance, the car turned into a circular driveway with a huge fountain in the middle and cherubs adorning the façade. A gentleman in a butler's uniform opened the car door and welcomed him to their facility.

"I am Roger Flounder. Please follow me, sir. I'll get your bags later."

Raymond acknowledged him with a nod and proceeded up the stairs. The doors opened onto a huge foyer. The light reflecting off the white marble floor illuminated the entrance and accented the large floral arrangement sitting in the middle of a gold gilded French provincial table. Raymond thought he had walked into a hotel, not a sanatorium. *This place looks impressive. I wonder where they hide all the loonies?*

Miss Cummings, Dr. Debrinski's secretary, greeted Raymond with an extended handshake. "We were anxiously awaiting your arrival, Mr. Miller. Your father wrote us requesting your stay and we are obliged to fulfill his wishes. He's a fine gentleman who contributes to many good causes."

Raymond snickered and wondered *how much this contribution cost him*, but kept quiet and followed Miss Cummings into an office. The cherrywood paneling supported the built-in bookshelves that lined the circumference of the room. Books were shelved in perfect rows. The presence of authority screamed from the walls. Raymond experienced the same feelings when he entered his father's library.

"Please have a seat, Mr. Miller; Dr. Debrinski will be here shortly."

Cummings left the room. Being too restless to sit, Ray decided to browse around the doctor's collection of books. He reached for Sigmund Freud's *Psychoanalysis*, Emil Kraepelin's textbook *Psychiatry*, and Paul Dubois's book *The Psychic Treatment of Mental Diseases*. *If this is some of the material Dr. Debrinski reads, he must excel in his profession. I still don't know how this is going to impact me.* Suddenly, he heard the door knob turn and quickly took a seat in the leather high back chair.

"Well, well, so this is my good friend's son, Raymond Miller, Jr. So glad to meet you."

Dr. Debrinski walked into the room with an extended hand. He gestured for Raymond to take a seat.

"Your father wrote me about a certain predicament you are in. He believes your excessive drinking caused the problem."

Ray displayed agitation. "That's not true. I can control my drinking. I only had a few drinks the day of the accident. What caused the problem was the lady standing in the middle of the street. I just didn't see her and didn't know I hit her. My father is so worried I might ruin his reputation that he sends me here."

Dr. Debrinski recognized Ray's anger and resentment.

"I can help you, Ray, if you let me. Your dad and I go back to our college days at Harvard and I owe him a favor. I also think you will benefit from our program. We have strict rules at Rosemont and they must be followed or you'll be asked to leave. For the first three months, you cannot leave the premises. We will be treating you for alcohol abuse and we don't want any outside temptations until you become equipped to handle them. You will receive ongoing therapy to find the root of your problems. You are expected to maintain a job in the sanatorium and attend all therapy sessions. You will receive a demerit for every expectation not met. If you receive five, you'll be sent packing. During the fourth month, you can leave the premises for a day, but only if accompanied by a worker. At the fifth and sixth month, you can leave daily to look for a job and try to reintegrate back into the community, while maintaining sobriety. If successful, you will be discharged at the end of the sixth month. If not, we make a new assessment to decide your fate."

Ray cringed at the words. *I guess I'll go along with this program to make my father happy and then make my way to the big city*, he thought.

After their chat, Dr. Debrinski summoned Gus, the ward worker, to take Raymond to his room. They climbed one flight of stairs and walked down a long narrow hall. Gus opened the door to room 111 and Raymond followed him into a stark white area that claimed one bed, nightstand, lamp, and a dresser shoved against the wall. *How sterile this place looks*, thought Ray. He ran to the window with a venetian blind and rolled it up to look outside. The eyes of the cherubs smiled back, as the fountain came into focus. The room wasn't cozy, but adequate.

First on Raymond's schedule was a medical exam. This didn't ruffle his feathers as much as the psychological testing. He demanded to know, "What are these bullshit pictures supposed to reveal?" He sat in Debrinski's office feeling like a plucked chicken on display. The doctor recognized that every time Raymond's performance was challenged, he reacted with outbursts. *Where was all his anger coming from? Getting him to discuss what it was like growing up in his household or interaction with friends is a challenge. He keeps his emotions suppressed.* The first two sessions elicited few words. He had nothing to offer about himself. At the next meeting, Raymond wiggled uncomfortably and often shrugged his shoulders. Finally, Dr. Debrinski talked forcefully of notifying Mr. Miller that nothing was being accomplished. The volcano erupted. Raymond's anger rolled off his tongue like a dragon spewing fire.

"Dad won't care unless it interferes with his life. My parents were seldom home when I was young. They traveled or went to campaign functions. My father didn't show much emotion. He seldom offered encouragement or compliments. He expected the best performance, yet did little to reinforce it. I remember making second place in the spelling bee and he was mad because I wasn't the winner. He never came to see me in school plays or sporting events. My mother showed affection but was pulled away by my father. Life was lonely and I grew up thinking there was something wrong with me."

When the session ended, he ran to his room shaking terribly. He felt like a train hit him against the wall. His defenses were down. *Debrinski provoked me into divulging my private thoughts. I need a drink to calm down.* He ran to his suitcase and found the cough medicine bottle hidden in a compartment that Gus overlooked when inspecting his bags. The clear liquid vodka went down smoothly. *Ah, that feels better.* The shaking of his hands subsided and he returned the bottle to its private domain.

After that outbreak, the sessions became easier. Raymond opened up about his life as an adolescent.

"The only thing that gave me comfort was food. The different tastes and textures added warmth to my life. So when I was unhappy, I ate a lot. The children at school teased me as my body ballooned. They called me 'porky,' 'tub of lard,' and 'chunk.' One day Steve Maroon said, 'oink, oink,' as I passed him in the school lunch room and all the kids laughed. I felt so ugly and defeated that I took a punch at him. I got reported, sent to the principal's office, and my parents were called. I was embarrassed over the incident, but I found it was my bad behavior that got my father's attention. After that episode, I became a loner to eliminate the torment. When my father ignored me or yelled that my grades weren't good enough for a councilman's son, I hid in my room as a youngster and later picked a spot at the bar as an adult."

Dr. Debrinski listened to Raymond's stories and events during his formative years that brought him so much unhappiness. No judgment was ever passed. Debrinski explained to Raymond that feeling rejection by his parents, and enduring loneliness placed him in a hostile and frightening environment. The result was anxiety. His defense was drinking to dull the pain.

Finally, Raymond thought, *this stocky, kind-looking doctor with wired rim spectacles propped on his nose and gray fuzz circling his bald head actually understands me.* Debrinski remembered what his mentor Paul Dubois wrote: "The goal of treatment was to make the patient master of himself." He concluded that if Raymond gained control of his life, he would move ahead and achieve his wildest dreams. But for him to stop drinking, he needed to feel worthy and secure as a person. *If I can get him to understand and interpret his feelings and needs, then Raymond can start developing positive relationships. This will be the treatment plan.* Dr. Debrinski sat back in his leather chair with a smile on his face feeling satisfied with his affirmation.

Raymond's life was not just attending therapy, he was also responsible for keeping his room clean and clothes washed. But it was his job in the library that gave him a spark of excitement. He researched in some law books to obtain information on cases pertaining to burglaries for his new friend, Danny Distoe. Raymond kept to himself most of the time, because he didn't feel comfortable around other residents. Danny was different. He had an appetite for learning and liked to debate controversial topics. Danny was only seventeen when he got into trouble with the law for petty theft. His father, a prominent New York banker, persuaded the judge to send him to Rosemont for treatment instead of jail. Danny wanted to know what the standard punishment was for a poor thief instead of a rich kid. Since Raymond was the librarian, he did the research. When he had time to read the briefs, he devoured the information on court hearings and verdicts. He felt the power of a lawyer over his clients. A person's future was in the hands of his attorney and the need for good and accurate research for court presentation was an art, not just a profession. Raymond read the cases to Danny and they discussed the tactics and outcomes. Raymond was enthralled with his new interests and decided to visit New York University Law School on his first visit to the city. *Won't Dr. Debrinski be surprised with my decision?*

Raymond's life at the sanatorium was orderly and quietly regimented. Once removed from his stressful environment, Raymond didn't need extra food for contentment and was satisfied with the meals provided. Soon the pounds came off and Raymond felt like a new person. He made progress in the therapy sessions and felt the load of his world become lighter, as the layers of resentment peeled away. He no longer needed a crutch and his desire for alcohol waned. He was indeed ready to visit Manhattan.

Raymond paced the foyer floor waiting for Gus to get the car and start their journey into the city. *What's taking Gus so long? I've been cooped up in this place for three months. I need to leave.* Just as Raymond was getting riled, he heard the horn honk and ran out of the building.

"Let's get out of here, Gus. I've got a great day planned. First, my appointment with Mr. Davis, the Admissions Director at the University, is at 10:00 a.m. He'll probably take me on a tour of the campus and then discuss the process required for applying to law school. I hope my transcripts from Wayne University are sufficient. Where will we meet after my interview?"

Gus thought a moment. "There is a little restaurant called Derby's on Sixth Avenue, a few blocks away from the main entrance. I'll be waiting there for you. Don't disappoint me."

"What do you mean by that?" Raymond felt hurt. "Don't you trust me? I'm not going to mess up now."

"Just be there."

"OK. OK."

Raymond went on about them going sightseeing before returning to Riverdale. He contemplated, *After my appointments, I want to make the most of this day. I'm not going to let Gus get on my nerves. Just think; one more month, I dump him and come back alone.*

Raymond returned at noon and found Gus sitting in a booth with a cup of coffee, reading the newspaper.

"Do you mind if we have lunch here? I'm starved," Raymond asked.

"What did you do for two hours?"

"It takes time, Gus, to look around the school and dormitories. Mr. Davis had some interruptions and then we talked about the requirements for being admitted. I still have a few classes to complete before entering law school. I feel positive about this meeting."

After lunch, they did the typical tours. Raymond was excited about reaching the top of the Empire State Building and having a panoramic view of New York. Next, they went to see the majestic lady holding her torch. The March winds sent a chill through Gus as he waited for Raymond to descend from the top of the Statue of Liberty. "We need to head back before it gets too late, and I'm cold." Raymond was disappointed because he wanted to see the night lights of Times Square and Broadway but went back without an argument. *It's better to stay on Gus's good side.* On the return drive, Raymond sat in awe reviewing the day. "Gus, I know this city holds the key to my future."

When Raymond arrived back to his room, he knew he had to perform a hard task: pick up the phone and call his dad. His father sent a check each month for his room and board, but never attempted to contact him. His mother sent a note periodically to give an update on what was happening back home. This time his call wasn't for getting out of trouble. It was for help to become the successful son his father wanted. When Mr. Miller answered the phone and heard his son's voice, there was silence. Raymond explained his plans to his father and wanted to know the direction to take in obtaining his transcripts and giving the private information needed for the application, such as an address for his residence. Mr. Miller felt his eyes fill with moisture. He couldn't believe his son wanted to become a lawyer, but knew he had to be careful about not revealing his son's whereabouts.

"Let me tell you the necessary steps to take with filling out your application. I will get you a New York resident address. There will be no mention of Rosemont. Write self-employed for your father's employment. I will pay your tuition and rent. You need a job to pay for books and food. Don't make any reference to your family home in Detroit. All communications will go through the New York residence. I will obtain your college transcripts and send them to you. Son, the day you left for the sanatorium, Detective Pierce came snooping around asking questions and wanting to speak to you. He also wanted to inspect your car. I told him you left the state to attend college and took your vehicle. I pleaded with him to quit the investigation and Pierce's boss confirmed the request. The case was closed. However, if you decide to come back or ignite any suspicion, your future plans could be destroyed."

"I understand, dad, but I never want to return to Detroit. In New York City lies my destiny."

Raymond followed his father's advice and filled out the application as directed. He submitted it along with the transcripts his father had sent. Now he had to wait.

Two more months and I'll be released from Rosemont, thought Raymond. *I must find housing and a part-time job. That's what I'll do on my next two visits to the city.* He pounded the pavement inquiring about a sales position, or a waiter, clerk, or janitor's job, but it was always the same answer: "You need experience or we don't have the money to hire at this time." Discouraged, Raymond sat down at the counter of Derby's to order a sandwich. Suddenly, he heard two people arguing in the back. One yelled, "I quit," and threw down his apron. The owner came out of the kitchen angry and picked up the apron to wrap around his waist. "Good riddance to that hothead," he said to Raymond. Quickly, Raymond responded.

"Are you going to need some help?"

"Can you cook?"

Raymond lied and said "Sure." The owner threw him the apron and said, "My name is Walt; now start working." He couldn't believe he landed the job as short order cook in a restaurant only two blocks away from the University.

On the weekend, he answered an ad for a walk-up studio in an area called Greenwich Village only a few blocks away from his job and school. A luxurious place it was not, but light came through the dirty window turning the dingy room into a tolerable living space. His Murphy bed folded up leaving an area for a couch, table, and lamp. His no-frill room at Rosemont prepared him for his no-frill apartment.

Spring brought early blooms to the perennials planted on the grounds of the sanatorium and Raymond was almost sad to leave the surroundings to which he had become accustomed, but most of all he would miss Dr. Debrinski. He had become the father figure that was missing in his life. He would no longer have the debates with Danny and guidance from big brother Gus. Raymond hashed over in his head, *I have to grow up and be on my own some time. It might as well be now.* He shook Dr. Debrinski's hand good-bye.

"We're proud of you, Raymond. You certainly came a long way. You are our first resident to be accepted into NYU's Law School. Good luck in the 1936 fall semester." Raymond's face beamed when he recalled receiving the letter of acceptance last week. Debrinski continued, "Remember just one thing; don't take that first drink, because you might not be able to stop."

Raymond gave him a condescending smile as if to say, *Don't worry. I don't have a drinking problem.*

As Mr. Potts placed his luggage in the trunk, Raymond entered the waiting car. This was the end of the Riverdale journey and Raymond would now embark on a new life. Dr. Debrinski watched through the window, as Mr. Potts pulled out of the driveway to deliver Raymond to his new apartment. There was one troubling thought going through the doctor's mind. *I have my doubts that Raymond can maintain his sobriety. If life's pressures become too intense, I wonder if this young man will return.*

CHAPTER 13

▼

THE BIRTH

Cleaning became Becky's virtue even though keeping a six-room flat in perfect condition was a hardship on her body. She washed the kitchen and bathroom floors on her knees, against doctor's orders. Her wringer washer was in the basement, so to save wear and tear on her leg, she declared Monday washday and stayed downstairs most of the day, only taking a lunch break with Rena. She soaked clothes in one tub and washed another load in her machine. Through the double wringer they were pushed and dumped into the rinse water of the second tub. The task completed, Becky fed the wash through the wringer again making it ready to hang on the clothesline. In the summer, she climbed up and down the stairs to the backyard so her clothes could dry in the fresh air under the radiant sun. Her leg became inflamed after washday, but that didn't stop Becky. The abuse continued. If the clothes needed starching, she would boil the starch on a burner in the basement and place it on the collars of the shirts. Becky stood on her feet to iron all the clothes and bedding. The dampness of the room caused her leg to draw and pain set in. When she complained to the doctors about the intensity, they offered her medication that made her drowsy. Becky complained to Dr. Palmer, "I can't take these pills and take care of my daughter."

She threw them away and endured the anguish.

When she started to feel nausea in the mornings, Becky thought it was due to fatigue, lack of sleep, and hard work. However, after two months and no period, she made an appointment with an obstetrician. He confirmed her fears. She was pregnant. Becky screamed, "I can't have this baby. Dr. Palmer warned me not to have any more children."

"Calm down, calm down," reassured Dr. Bliss. We can get you through this. I'll confer with your other physicians and find the best way to handle your pregnancy."

"No, you don't understand. We don't have the money for another child." Becky ran out of the office crying.

When she returned home she ran upstairs to talk this over with her friend.

"What am I going to do, Mary? Rena is seven and a handful. The teachers at the school report she sits and stares out the window most of the day and doesn't want to participate in class. She's a loner and doesn't make friends easily. Nate went down to two jobs and we are just getting by. I no longer have baby items and would need to start from scratch. My stepmother won't help. Sometimes she talks to me and other times I don't exist. Should I just jump off the stove and see if I can abort the baby?"

Mary took Becky's hand.

"You need to think straight. First, if you try anything stupid and injure yourself, it will cost Nate more money for doctor bills. My family is here to help with the new baby, so it won't be that difficult for you."

Becky felt better after talking to Mary and wiped her tears.

"Now I need to break the news to Nate."

"If I know Nate, he will be overjoyed about having another child."

"I hope you're right. Maybe Rena will be excited to be a big sister and help out," Becky said.

As she walked downstairs, she wondered if delivering the baby would be difficult due to her internal damage from the accident. That evening she broke the news to Nate and Rena. Nate grabbed Becky and gave her a big hug.

"I'm so happy, but what about your health? I wish we could hire a nanny to help you. We just don't have the extra money."

"Don't worry, Nate. Dr. Bliss reassured me that he will take extra precautions. He ordered me to take rest periods through-out the day. Mary promised to help with the baby. I don't know what I would do without her."

Nate and Becky looked at Rena to see her reaction. There wasn't much. Nate asked, "Are you going to be the big sister, Rena and help mommy out?" Rena shrugged her shoulders, as if to say *I don't know what to think or what I will do.*

During the pregnancy, Becky gained only twenty-five pounds and tried not to exert herself. She took rest periods throughout the day. When Bertha called for Becky to come over and make Sabbath dinner, Becky refused.

"I'm feeling too tired to get on the bus with Rena to travel to your house and then stand on my feet all day to cook."

Bertha hung up. Becky felt guilty, but too tired to care.

Becky felt huge in her last month as she packed her suitcase to prepare for delivery. Rena asked sarcastically,

"Where am I going to stay this time, while you're in the hospital?"

"You're seven years old now, Rena, and since it is October you need to be in school. When you come home, go up and see Aunt Mary. She'll prepare dinner and you can do your homework. At night, go downstairs to sleep in your bedroom. Her daughter, Marilyn, will stay with you. This routine will only last for two weeks."

Just as Rena was about to object, the phone rang.

"Becky, it is Lilly. I have some good news for you. I eloped. Steve and I are married."

"You've done what? How could you not invite us to your wedding?"

"Becky, you're ready to deliver a baby; how could you come to Chicago?"

"You could have married here. I never even met your husband."

"No, I didn't want any other members of the family at my wedding. However, you're going to meet Steve real soon, because we're moving to Detroit in about two weeks."

"Oh, I'm so excited, Lilly. Why don't you stay with us until you find a house?"

"No, you have enough going on with the new baby coming, but we'll look for a place near you. Steve's company is putting us up at the Book-Cadillac for a week until we find housing. I'll see you soon, big sister, and good luck if your baby arrives before we do."

Becky was so excited she couldn't wait to tell Nate.

"What are you so happy about, mother?" questioned Rena.

"Come here and I will tell you and your father."

Nate was happy for his wife, because she needed family around her who weren't always trying to abuse her. With the new baby coming, having Lilly nearby would be a comfort.

"By the way, Nate, I went to see Dr. Bliss today and he thinks because I'm carrying the child so low in my stomach that we might be having a boy. I thought we should name him David, after your mother."

"I don't want a brother. I would rather have a sister."

"It doesn't matter what you want; we take what God gives us. Let's pray the baby is healthy," explained Becky.

Rena ran to her room in a huff.

"Becky, I think we should pick a girl's name just in case. If we have a daughter, let's call her Dena."

October 12, 1941, approached and Rena's school prepared for the Columbus Day celebration. However, there was a bigger celebration at the Abroms' house, when Becky's water broke at 10:00 p.m. on the 11th just before Nate departed for work. He called Sanders to say he was taking his wife to deliver the baby.

Nate ran upstairs to get Mr. Wilbur to drive them to the hospital and their daughter came down to stay with Rena. Five hours later a red-faced screaming little girl came into the world and Becky and Nate laughed. It was no David. Rena had gotten her wish.

Becky chose to nurse her baby. The medical profession advocated a healthier child with mother's milk. Nate called all the relatives and friends to let them know, but Bertha's tone was indifferent. The future relationship between the Abroms and Hoobermans proved to be on and off with Bertha pulling the strings. If Bertha was mad or unhappy with Becky, she made up stories and instigated trouble between the half-siblings, so Sammy, Richie, and Rona stayed away. "Your sister doesn't want you kids at her house. She claims your clothes look dilapidated and she doesn't want her neighbors gossiping about the way you dress." For some reason, which Becky didn't understand, Bertha had the power to accomplish the destruction of a whole family. Yet, Jakie and Lilly were never under her control.

When Becky and Nate arrived home from the hospital with their little bundle, Mary was right there to help.

"Let Aunt Mary take this precious package."

The baby slept in Becky and Nate's bedroom in a cradle borrowed from the Wilburs. This way, Rena wouldn't wake up when the baby cried and Becky could feed Dena in bed. It was hard when Nate left for work at night and Becky was all alone with the two girls. She knew, however, if there was a problem, help was close by. Becky's neighbors were her replacement family.

CHAPTER 14

▼

BAD NEWS—GOOD NEWS

With Becky home from the hospital and Nate having given up his third job, the blanket of despair peeled away and some normalcy returned to the household. However, turmoil erupted in their community as alarming news came over the airwaves. The political climate in Europe was changing drastically. Talk fluttered through the synagogues, the Jewish Community Center, and even the Schvitz, the public hot baths. Nate read in the Jewish newspapers that European Jews were in danger. "Adolf Hitler, leader of the Nazi party, ordered the round-up of all German Jews. The Nazis forced them to wear armbands with the yellow Star of David for identity purposes and commanded the Jews to leave their homes for containment in a ghetto." Most people said, "How can this be?" They rationalized that this was temporary and soon everything would return to normal, but it never happened.

Everyone listened to the radio for updates on the European front. Nate called, "Becky, it is 6:00 p.m. Let's listen to Walter Winchell." They listened intently as dinner was served in the kitchen. On September 1,1939, breaking news blared through the wires: "Hitler's army crossed the border into Poland. This move forces England and France into war with Germany. Europe's World War II has begun."

Panic spread in every Jewish community. Families were receiving letters from friends and relatives in Europe depicting the crisis. Reports from the New York Yiddish dailies revealed that "hundreds of Jewish civilians were massacred by Nazi soldiers." The Jewish Chronicle's headline read, "Influential Jewish people substantiate that the Jews of Warsaw were gathered together and placed into a ghetto like animals pushed into a corral."

"I don't get it," complained Nate. "Why doesn't our government look into these allegations?"

What he didn't realize was, according to reports, "over 100 anti-Semitic organizations pumped hate propaganda throughout American society and people including some Congress members viewed Jews as a menace. The State Department claimed they needed more proof of the calamities and that the stories received were rumors built on hysteria." As time lapsed, American Jews felt helpless but continued to listen, to read, and to pray.

Becky tried to distract Nate from listening to all the depressing news. "Let's walk to the Avalon Theatre and see the new Fred Astaire and Eleanor Powell movie: *The Broadway Melody of*

1940. We need relief from the disturbing reports coming from overseas. Mrs. Klein, from next door, saw it and said the Cole Porter music is great. Escape to Hollywoodland is what I need as I watch Astaire dance around the room and dream he's twirling toward me."

"All right, Becky; I see you're smitten with him. Let's go. Besides, I can watch the newsreel before the movie. Maybe we can learn more about the Nazi advances in Europe."

Rena stayed with Mrs. Klein while they went to an early show. When the Movie-Tone news went on, they both sat with wide open eyes, and neither was tempted to take one mouthful of popcorn.

"The summer of 1940 and Germany is making gains. Within one week, Holland surrenders, then Belgium, and Luxembourg."

However, the audience's attention was focused on "Germany's new Panzer armies slicing through and crumbling French defenses at Sedan as they fought to the river's edge and then crossed over the Meuse River. This was accomplished in three days."

"My gosh," Nate whispered to Becky. "The dirty Nazis, their conquests are more successful than I thought."

Before Nate could utter another word, the music started and Becky was thankful for a diversion. She had seen enough sorrow on the screen. Fred Astaire, wearing his dancing shoes, dipped Powell into his embrace. She swayed to the music as he sang, "I've Got My Eyes For You." All this tenderness put Becky in a romantic mood, as she nestled up to her husband. Nate watched the tapping feet, but his head couldn't lose the thunderous sound of marching boots from the newsreel. Thud, thud, tap, tap. Nate's head was spinning. No matter how he tried to concentrate on the stars, the vision of Nazi storm troopers crossing the European borders reappeared. The power of this visual imagery brought anguish to his heart.

Two significant surprises entered into the Abroms' life in 1941. First, it was the birth of a daughter instead of the son the doctor had predicted. The second shock that moved the country was announced when Nate was in the kitchen making hot tea and Becky was in the bedroom changing Dena's diaper.

"America is being attacked," Nate shouted, "Becky, I can't believe what I just heard."

He repeated the story to her, as she came running into the kitchen with the baby in tow.

"The Japanese bombed Pearl Harbor. We're under attack."

On December 7, 1941, World War II began for the United States.

Neighborhood talk was rampant. People were scared to think how the war would affect their families, as young soldiers were sent overseas. Jakie Hooberman was one of them and Becky was afraid she might lose her only full-blood brother. Trying to keep her mind off the war, she became consumed with caring for her newborn and trying to appease Rena. Although, her patience was wearing thin. When the pain in her leg set in, she would release her frustrations.

"Rena, why don't you find friends to play with? Close the refrigerator door with the handle; your finger prints are on it. Don't make a mess in the living room with your toys."

The venting continued. The more Becky preached, the quieter Rena became and she retreated to her room or misbehaved again. "Don't pick on her so much," Nate begged, but Becky and Rena were always at odds. As Dena grew into a toddler, Nate or Aunt Mary babysat more in the afternoons, while Becky volunteered at the synagogue packaging canned goods, making bandages, and shipping clothes overseas. Becky did her share for Uncle Sam.

Nate was past the age limit to enlist, so he volunteered as a neighborhood air-raid warden and attended meetings before work. Bomb shelters were built. People were taught how to protect themselves and follow procedures in case of air attacks. Rena and Dena would run to the window to watch their father leave all dressed up in his white metal helmet, armband, and carrying a gas mask ready to patrol the neighborhood streets during emergency drills. "Daddy looks so brave," boasted Rena to her mother.

The Wilburs contributed to the war effort by opening their home to servicemen on furlough. Dena loved to visit upstairs and meet the men in uniform who made a fuss over her dimples and curls. Sometimes they would hold her in their arms and want a picture of them together. "Don't be a nuisance, Dena," Becky warned as she saw her daughter heading towards the stairs one Sunday afternoon at dinner time. Aunt Mary always reassured Becky that her daughter brought so much laughter to the soldiers. She reminded them of Shirley Temple, the little dimpled darling of Hollywood.

Finally, in March, 1942, proof came in about the atrocities taking place in Eastern Europe.

"Listen to this, Becky. This information is coming right from the chief representative for the Relief Activities of the American Jewish Joint Distribution Committee." Nate continued reading from the Jewish publications. "'The representative was an eyewitness and estimated that 240,000 Jews had been massacred in the Ukraine alone and the slaughtering was continuing in full fury.' Still nothing is being done. I can't believe it."

What Nate didn't know was that it would take another year before reports of gassing were revealed. The committee transmitted its alarming find in May, 1942:

"A special vehicle, maintaining a gas chamber, was employed to load ninety people at a time for suffocation. On average, 1000 people were gassed daily. The conclusion was formed: Germany had set out to exterminate all the Jews in Europe."

Finally, the State Department began to inquire into the massacres of Jews in Eastern Europe and the American Jewish press released the news. Mass protests and organized demonstrations began, but it wasn't enough to get the United States immigration to change its quotas. No additional Jewish immigrants were allowed into the country to escape their demise in Europe.

Within the year, news worsened: "The Jewish ghettos population decreased, as people were packed onto trains heading for concentration camps."

Gossip flourished in the neighborhood; so many people had their own tragic stories. Becky witnessed Mrs. Goldberg's war jitters as she waited in line at Kramer's butcher shop with a meat coupon in hand. Coupons were issued by President Roosevelt's Office of Price Administration (OPA) to ensure an ample supply of food for civilians, allied soldiers, and the growing population of war refugees. Fancy cuts of meat were scarce, but inexpensive cuts were still available with government coupons. After the butcher wrapped her meat, Becky rushed home to give Nate a blow-by-blow description of what took place in the shop earlier today:

"Mrs. Goldberg passed out in Mr. Kramer's store today, as she was buying hamburger meat. The news about gassing Jews came over the little radio he kept on the top shelf against the wall. She hadn't heard from her sister in Poland for over a month and the thought of Sadie and her family being among the gassed victims was more then poor Mrs. Goldberg could bear."

Nate shrugged his shoulders and shook his head after hearing the story. The spiraling events in Europe brought him nightmares. He remembered the prejudice and persecution suffered as a youth in Romania. He no longer heard from any relatives who remained in his village and wondered as to their fate.

Becky felt the hardship of war when she encountered a shortage of food at Joe's grocery store. Often she waited in line to buy sugar and butter. After coming home exhausted from shopping, Becky collapsed on the couch while explaining, "Nate, the bread on the store shelves is coming in not sliced. Joe said the war is causing factories to 'conserve manpower'."

The big change came to Detroit when factory workers stopped building cars and switched to producing war materials.

Michigan became the "Arsenal of Democracy." Some people profited from the war effort, while others lost out. Nate's karma changed in 1943 and he became one of the lucky ones. He found his fortune, but it was short-lived.

CHAPTER 15

▼

THE BUSINESS DEAL

Nate got off the bus on a balmy May morning, hurrying to reach his house and tell Becky about his great business opportunity. He wondered how she would react when he announced he quit Sanders. His brother told him not to quit: "It's a secure job, Nate, and with your expenses you need the security."

However, when Nate was refused a raise, he saw his opportunities limited. So after eighteen years, he said, "goodbye." On his walk home, he inhaled the sweet smell of the lilacs and admired the splash of reds, yellows, and purples from the tulips and irises. How he loved the sprouting of the spring flowers. *Someday I'm going to have my own flower garden.* He climbed the front stairs, opened the door and yelled, "Becky, are you home?"

Becky was in the kitchen baking when Nate walked in. He started to explain how he quit his two jobs to begin a new career. She put the mixing spoon down, sat on the closest chair, and stared in amazement.

"How can you just quit? How are we going to live?"

"I never let you down yet, Becky. Now listen to me; you won't believe what happened. Sam came to me at lunch and told me he had a connection with a friend whose father owns a slaughter house on Kirby Street. He has access to meat and the supply is unlimited but they need a butcher that can run a retail business. Sam knows that I worked in a butcher shop before, so he approached me to take advantage of this once-in-a-lifetime opportunity. I jumped at the deal. People are waiting in lines for meat and we will have the goods to give them. This is my chance to make a lot of money."

"You didn't even ask me first."

"There was no time. They found a store and wanted to lease it right away."

"What about a contract to sign and what would be your split?"

"First, I trust Sam; he's my best friend. Sam, his friend George, and I shook hands and that's our agreement. We buy the meat from George's father and Sam and I split the profits after all the expenses are paid. We can't lose."

Nate's foolproof business deal was profitable and the money came pouring in. Customers came from all over when their local butchers couldn't fill the orders. Long lines formed at the shop and Becky served as cashier. They plopped her on a high stool to keep the pressure off her leg, while she kept the cash register ringing. Becky tried to keep the regular customers happy by offering extra services. If a child cried, she gave a cookie. If an elderly person couldn't stand so long, she brought a chair. If someone was short a coupon, she let them bring it in the next time. Unfortunately, the good times did not last forever. When the war ended in 1945, the meat shortage ended. People returned to their convenient butcher shops, forgetting the Abroms' kindness. The crucial problem was the dishonesty of their meat supplier. As the demand for meat increased, George and his father thought Nate and Sam were making too much money. So they squeezed for more money by increasing the wholesale prices. When they complained to George, he told them to find another slaughterhouse if they weren't happy. Nate knew that their golden goose was cooked and when their business decreased after the war, they decided to end the agreement. Nate went back to baking, but not for Sanders. He found a job at an independent bakery shop, where he was the sole baker. His salary increased significantly. Sam returned to Sanders. Over the year and a half of being self-employed, Nate had put away a nest egg, but that was not to last.

CHAPTER 16

▼

DEATH REVISITED

The Abroms felt defeated after the butcher shop closed. Becky moped around the house wondering how all that hard work abruptly ended. Lilly stopped over daily to check on her sister and tried to cheer her up. She brought bagels, butter horns or other deli treats. However, this morning Lilly came with great news and hoped her sister could share her joy.

"I've been dying to tell you all day, but I needed to tell Steve first."

"What is it, my darling?"

"Becky, I'm going to have a baby."

She hugged Lilly. "I'm so happy for you. When is the baby due?"

"Not until next fall."

Becky could tell from Lilly's face that something was worrying her. "Lilly, is there a problem?"

"I'm worried that I can't travel as much with Steve during my pregnancy. Traveling for business doesn't concern me, but Steve likes to take frequent trips to Las Vegas and I want to go with him."

Becky saw how much Lilly was in love with her husband and tended to overlook his excessive gambling and selfishness. She discussed Steve's gambling debts many times with Nate. "How can we help, Lilly?"

"Just be supportive and don't butt in."

Lilly traveled with Steve until her seventh month and then quit because of her size and swollen legs. When Irena was born, Lilly was elated that Steve was in town; however, having a baby didn't keep him around the house more. It just meant that Lilly couldn't be with him. When Irena reached the age of one, Steve wanted to take Lilly on a trip to California and Lilly had to find a nanny to care for the baby, but she didn't trust just anyone and the cost was high for a two-week vacation. Becky listened to her dilemma and offered to babysit with Irena.

"I can't impose on you."

"Nonsense. Let me discuss it with Nate first and if he agrees then it's settled."

"Oh, you're a doll," and she went over to hug her sister. "By the way, I want you to see something." Lilly unbuttoned her blouse and slipped it off her shoulder.

"What do you think this is?"

Becky took her finger, rubbed it across Lilly's shoulder, and felt a lump about the size of a walnut.

"I don't know, Lilly. I would have a doctor look at it before you go on your trip."

"I know. I already made an appointment for this week."

Lilly left and Becky sat down with a cup of coffee and started to worry that the lump might be a malignant tumor. When she told Nate, he reassured her that a little lump is nothing to worry about and the doctor will probably tell her to have it removed. Nate agreed to have Irena stay with them in spite of the strain on his wife.

"Becky, don't you take on too much, especially with all your pain?"

"I'll do anything to make Lilly happy."

There. I'm done packing, Lilly thought in relief. She bent down to close her second cardboard suitcase. *Now all I need is to finish packing for Irena.* Suddenly, the door-bell rang. Lilly ran to open the door and saw Becky peeking through the window.

"Becky, what are you doing here?"

"I came to see if I can help pack some of Irena's toys and start taking them to my house. You only have two days before leaving."

"I'm so excited. Steve and I really appreciate you taking the baby."

"No problem; but Lilly, are you sure you should leave before removing that lump?"

"I told you, Becky, I went to three doctors. Two said leave it alone, it's nothing, and only one said to remove it. When I get back from California, I'll decide what to do. Don't look so worried; it's nothing."

"All right; it's your decision."

The next two weeks, while Lilly and Steve were gone, Becky had her hands full. Irena cried at night because she missed her mother, and Rena and Dena fought for the baby's attention or complained.

"Mom, the baby's diaper is dirty. Mom, Irena is into my toys."

Becky was reaching the point of exhaustion. Consoling Irena and keeping peace between her two girls was a task, but the late hours at night cleaning brought Becky to her wits' end. *One more day and my sister comes home.*

When Lilly and Steve arrived the next evening to pick up the baby, Becky was alarmed that Lilly looked so pale and tired.

"Lilly, you just had a vacation; why do you look so weary?"

"We did a lot of running around and Steve made business contacts, so wining and dining was part of the agenda. I'm exhausted and also worried."

Lilly removed her shirt to show Becky the lump that was once the size of a walnut had grown to the size of an orange. Becky felt faint.

"How could it grow so fast in two weeks?"

"I don't know, Becky. I'm making an appointment with Dr. Schlur right away. He was the doctor who wanted to remove it immediately."

Becky tried to hold back the tears. Nobody wanted to think it. Nobody wanted to say it. The memories still lingered of their mother's battle with cancer. Lilly's surgery was scheduled in two weeks. Becky wanted to be there, but Lilly needed her to care for the baby.

"Steve will be with me, Becky. Don't worry; everything will be fine."

After surgery, the tumor was sent to the laboratory for analyzing. Steve told the doctors to call him with the report. He didn't want his wife to know the news if it was bad. The report came back *malignant.* Steve wondered, *was the carnivorous savage running rampant throughout her body?* Dr. Schlur told him that only time would tell. Steve told Lilly they had no conclusive report about the tumor and Lilly told Becky that everything was fine. Lilly continued caring for her household and Irena as if nothing was wrong. Becky tried to believe she was fine, but something wasn't right.

"I don't know the whole story about Lilly's health," she confessed to Nate. As the months went by, Lilly got thinner. When Becky questioned her, she answered, "It must be my diet."

There was a heat wave in the summer of 1947. Jake was expected home from the army within the next three weeks. Dena would begin kindergarten in the fall and Rena would enter Durfee Junior High. With all this excitement, Lilly's downward health went unnoticed. After all, she kept saying, everything was fine. When the ambulance was called in the evening of August 24, Lilly was lying in bed in a coma. A neighbor came in to stay with Irena and Steve went with his wife. He knew he'd be saying goodbye. As the stretcher was wheeled into the hospital, a woman from Lilly's book club was waiting in the hospital for her son's hand to be stitched after a fall. She recognized Steve as he ran into the hospital with his wife. After an hour, she went to the nurse at the station and inquired about what happened to the patient that was brought in.

"The poor dear," replied the nurse. "She died about twenty minutes ago from complications of cancer."

The woman was taken aback. *I can't believe this happened to Lilly. I better call her sister and give my regrets.* However, Becky didn't know anything about her sister's critical condition. When the phone rang in the Abroms' household, Becky said, "I'll answer it," thinking it might be her brother announcing his arrival to Detroit. Becky picked up the receiver. "Hello."

"Is this Becky?"

"Yes."

"This is Charlotte Birkow, your sister's friend. I just called to give my condolences."

"What do you mean?"

"I'm sorry about the death of your sister. "

Becky froze. She tried walking towards Nate but her legs were numb, no movement, paralyzed. The receiver dropped and she let out a piercing scream. Nate heard the deafening sound and came running.

"Becky, what is it?"

"My sister is dead. Someone called me on the phone to tell me my sister is dead," she screamed over and over again.

Nate couldn't control her. He panicked and called Dr. Palmer at home.

"Dr. Palmer, this is Nathan Abrom. My wife received news her sister died and now she cannot walk and is screaming uncontrollably. "

"Mr. Abrom, take your wife to Receiving Hospital's psychiatric ward. I think she is having a nervous breakdown. I will call my good friend Dr. Shapiro to meet you there. He's an excellent psychiatrist."

Nate couldn't believe what was happening. *It's been ten years since her one-year hospital stay. Now she's going back. Will she recover from this ordeal?*

CHAPTER 17

▼

THE ENCOUNTER

Next month, I stop flipping hamburgers all day, thought Raymond as he shook the frying basket of French fries and wiped the sweat off his forehead. *Once school starts, I only have to work the dinner shift. I'm ready for the challenge of law school. Just thinking about NYU lifts my spirits. Taking this job at Derby's is obviously beneath my station in life but it pays the bills with some money to spare. I can't believe it's been four months since leaving Rosemont. I'm finishing the two required undergraduate classes and still doing fine on my own. I'll prove to father and Dr. Debrinski that, with time, I can succeed.*

Determined to make a good impression on the first day of school, Raymond placed his navy slacks, white shirt, and blue tie on the couch ready to slip on in the morning. While lying in deep thought, he remembered how his mother had taken him shopping for back-to-school clothes. *We're a long way from those days, Mother.* He fell asleep tasting the salty tears. The clock rang at 7:00 a.m. and startled Raymond. He wasn't used to early hours. His day at Rosemont began at nine. He jumped out of bed, showered, and dressed. His navy jacket completed the attire. He combed back his hair, indented a top wave, grabbed a piece of toast, and ran down the stairs. He walked briskly the few blocks to campus breathing the cool fall breeze, but missed the beds of colorful chrysanthemums he viewed from his window at Rosemont. Greenwich Village had cement and trees. When he opened the door to his first class, he pinched himself to prove that he wasn't dreaming.

The introductory classes were in criminal and corporate law, torts, civil procedure, and constitutional law. As Professor Jenkins said, "The way you learn the basics is to analyze the cases."

Professor Thomas brought excitement to a rather dull theory class by having his students learn case rulings and set precedence for different court decisions. Raymond excelled in the investigating assignments. Every afternoon after classes and before work, he entered the law library, sat at the same mahogany table near the card catalog, opened his books and did research.

After an hour he stretched and decided to take a break. As he glanced up, he noticed a striking blond sitting directly across the aisle. She looked up and saw him staring at her. Immediately, she returned to focus on her notebook. *I've got to meet that girl. She's a knockout.* Raymond contemplated how he would introduce himself. He was never attracted to any girl before, as he never thought he was good enough for the pretty ones. *All that therapy with Dr. Debrinski paid off,* he decided. *For the first time, I'm slim, handsome, and desirable. I have gained enough confidence to go over and say hello to that gal.* He slowly walked towards her after pretending to look up information in the card catalog.

"Excuse me. Are you in the law program at NYU? I see you're studying as hard as me."

"Yes, I am. And you are?"

"Oh, I'm sorry. I'm Raymond Miller, Jr."

"I'm Cindy Stranton."

"I think I've seen you in the hall at school," as he stretched the truth to continue the conversation. The other students started to give them looks and said "hush."

"Do you want to go for coffee? We can walk to Derby's. Besides, I think our talking is disturbing others."

Cindy agreed. "That would be nice; I could use a break."

They walked the few blocks and entered the eatery to find the place packed. "Let's grab that one vacant booth," suggested Raymond, as he followed Cindy to the back. Tiffany approached them and smiled when she saw it was Raymond with a girl. She didn't say a word about him working at the "joint." When Raymond first started at Derby's, Tiffany tried to flirt with him, but her aspirations weren't high enough for him. He knew she would always be a waitress until some man came along and proposed. *Stay clear of this broad,* he thought. *I want to meet someone with high status and beneficial to my career.*

Cindy's looks not only attracted Raymond, but the more she talked about her family and their estate on the Grand Concourse in the Bronx, the more appealing she became.

"After my second year of college, I plan to join my father's law firm, Stranton, Gross, and Stein."

Raymond had heard of that prestigious firm and knew they handled big cases. He looked at her puzzled.

"I thought it was three years for a degree."

"It is; but if I read the law cases and their rulings from the judge's recommended list and then take an oral test in court given by the judge, I can become a lawyer. You should think about doing the same thing."

"I don't know. Right now, I'm not thinking of short cuts. I need direction about what type of law to pursue. I envy the position of a Supreme Court Justice. That's the pinnacle of power and power is my goal."

Cindy liked Raymond's ambition and knew her father would, too. "Tell me about your family," she asked.

Raymond thought a moment and knew he had to stay clear of that discussion. *I can't tell her anything that happened in Detroit. I'll have to think of a rational family history for later.*

He managed to get out, "My parents do a lot of traveling. My father is a councilman in Detroit and is thinking of furthering his political career."

He was abrupt, thought Cindy. *I won't delve any further.* Raymond looked at his watch and realized he needed to start work in ten minutes. He admitted that he worked at Derby's to help with expenses. She just smiled and got up to leave.

"I hope I'll see you on campus or at the library," she said, and walked out the door. Raymond wasn't sure if he should pursue this relationship because he didn't want any distractions from school. However, he thought, *she could be an asset. Cindy's father has connections. If law is my future, then the Stranton family is the connection.* Raymond put on his apron and started working in the kitchen.

The next day, he couldn't wait to reach the library and meet Cindy. She wasn't there. He got his books out and started studying, but instead started fantasizing. *This is doing me no good. I see her beautiful oval face with a dimple on her chin, and small rounded hips that evolve from an eighteen inch waist. I can't go on.*

Finally, at the end of the week, Raymond walked into the library and found Cindy at the same table across from his favorite spot. He walked over.

"Do you mind if we study together?"

She nodded no. He grabbed a chair, spread his books, and they worked for three hours on law vocabulary. *Know the terminology, know procedure*; those were the words of the law professors throughout the semester. Time flew by and Raymond had only fifteen minutes to get to work. However, before he left, he asked Cindy for her telephone number. She replied, "I thought you'd never ask."

The semester was ending and preparing for final exams was imminent. Cindy and Raymond were known as the studying team and made plans to meet and quiz each other for their tests, if a convenient place could be found. Speaking too much was frowned upon in the library. Cindy lived in the dormitory and gentlemen weren't allowed past the parlor gathering area. Cindy thought there were too many people sitting on couches in deep discussion to give them an area to study. Raymond hesitated to ask, but out of desperation for a quiet place, he blurred out,

"You can come to my apartment and study. I can make coffee and we can quiz each other on the test questions. However, I'll understand if you say no. It's not proper for a single woman to come to a man's place."

Cindy didn't hesitate too long, when she replied: "That's a fine idea, Raymond." Raymond was surprised. He never thought she'd agree. They walked hand and hand to Raymond's walk-up. Cindy was anxious to see where he lived. She found it small, but neat. Of course, there was no room to be sloppy. The opened books lay on the floor. Their beverages rested on the coffee table and they sat on the small couch going over class notes. The nice part was they were alone.

Raymond was mesmerized by Cindy's sparkling blue eyes. He wanted to press his lips against hers and take her gently in his arms. *Wait*, he thought. *If I move too fast, I might scare her away*. He controlled himself and silently thought *I need to pick the right time*. When he saw it was getting late, he recommended they call it a day, so he could get to work. Cindy bent down and gave Raymond a peck goodbye on the cheek. That night, lying in bed, he concluded, *I think I'm falling in love and it has nothing to do with Cindy being rich. I miss every moment I'm away from her. Right after exams, I'm going to ask her for a date.*

He jumped out of bed to look in his cigar box and count his savings. *I have enough for two tickets to a play and dinner.*

The plan was to meet at Derby's right after their tests but before semester break. Raymond arrived first, hoping it wouldn't take Cindy too long to finish. After two cups of coffee, he saw her coming in the door.

"How do you think it went?"

"Pretty well," she replied. "I think all the studying paid off."

"Me too. Cindy, I know we're study partners, but how about seeing a play with me Saturday night?"

"I'd love to Raymond, except I'm going home for Thanksgiving. How about coming home with me?"

Raymond was taken back by the offer. He forgot about the holiday, because he had no place to go. He wasn't prepared to meet Cindy's parents yet. He thought about all the questions they might ask. "No thanks; I probably have to work if they keep the restaurant open. Besides, I can grab a meal here."

"Raymond, I don't want you to be alone."

He reached for her hand and gently squeezed it. She smiled and wanted to add, *I'll miss you.* Her thoughts were interrupted when Tiffany came to take their order. After rushing through lunch, Cindy realized she needed to leave for the train station. Raymond walked with her, hesitant to let her go. As they approached the track, she ran into his arms. He bent down and kissed her hard on the lips. She left his embrace and started toward the train. She turned and shouted,

"How about taking me to the ballet when I get back? It's *Swan Lake.*"

"I can't wait."

Raymond arrived at the restaurant ten minutes early and looked for his boss, Walt.

"How about putting me on the dinner shift for Thanksgiving?"

"We're not open for the holiday." Walt noticed Raymond's disappointment. "Did Cindy go home for the weekend?"

"Yeah, she invited me. I declined."

Walt didn't want to pry, but wondered why he didn't go. "Come to our house for turkey dinner. Midge won't mind if you can stand chattering kids.

"Well, I don't—"

"Come on. I won't take no for an answer."

Finally, Raymond gave in and accepted.

When he reached home late that evening, he picked up the phone to call his father. After two rings, he put the receiver down. What's the difference? He won't let me come home.

Raymond felt uneasy as he rang the doorbell to Walt and Midge's home on Washington Square. He thought: *I should be home with my family for the holiday, although I feel the Derby's employees are my family now.* Walt greeted him at the door, placed his arm around Raymond's shoulder and led him into the living room. The room was decorated modestly with a plaid couch, leather chair, and one smaller chair, probably for Midge. No fancy artifacts were displayed. Only a crucifix adorned the hallway wall. Three children ran into the room each asking questions to fill their curious minds. When Midge came in to greet him and announce dinner, Raymond welcomed the diversion.

Their daughter Josephine took her chair and her brothers Charles and Joseph found their spots around the large wooden table. Walt motioned for Raymond to sit near him. Midge was busy serving, but finally sat down directly across from her husband. Walt maintained the role of boss to Raymond; however, at home he showed a softer side. When Midge brought in the turkey, Walt rose to take the platter and start carving. With his belly hanging over his belt as if he swallowed a watermelon, Walt attacked the bird with precise direction and meticulous strokes. First, he cut the drumsticks, then the wings, until the fowl was completely carved. Each child requested his favorite part.

Walt laid each cut piece on a white platter trimmed with gold. All the holiday side dishes were in place.

"Please pass the stuffing," shouted eight-year-old Charles.

"I want the sweet potatoes," demanded four-year-old Joseph.

Josephine felt dignified at ten and quietly asked if someone could pass the cranberries. Midge took around the salad and string beans. After refusing a beer, Raymond watched Walt drink his with gusto. He envisioned the cool liquid flowing down his throat and knew how good it could feel. Raymond heard the noise around him but wasn't listening to the conversation. His mind was occupied with Cindy. Walt sensed this when Raymond didn't respond to his question on how his parents spent the holiday. His trance ended when the custard pudding and pumpkin pie were served. Feeling as stuffed as the bird, Raymond needed to walk and breathe some fresh air. He excused himself, thanked the family for their hospitality and left. Walt was puzzled. He never saw Raymond so preoccupied.

Raymond walked quickly back to the Village as the wind picked up. He thought, *it's too early to be so cold.* Picking up his coat collar for protection, he walked rapidly to his apartment. Out-of-breath, he climbed the stairs and heard the phone ring. Huffing and puffing, he quickly opened the door and went to grab the receiver. The ringing stopped. *I wonder if that was Cindy. I wish she would call. Why didn't I take her parents' phone number?* He picked up a book, but couldn't concentrate. He went to bed, but couldn't sleep. He looked at the clock: it was only ten. Suddenly, the phone rang. He reached for the receiver and prayed it was Cindy. When he heard her voice, he took a deep breath and exhaled with relief.

"How was your holiday, Raymond?"

They exchanged details of their dinner experience and shared the pain of not being together.

"Daddy wants to meet you. I told him maybe you'll come for Christmas."

"I'll be going home for Christmas," he said, not really believing it.

Raymond didn't know how long he could put Cindy off. He figured *I need more time before meeting Mr. Stranton.* Cindy felt rejected and wondered if Raymond were holding something back. She never asked. After they hung up, Cindy thought, *How well do I know this man? Can I trust him?* Raymond thought *I need accomplishments to prove myself worthy before meeting her father. I need to deserve Cindy's love. Meeting important people makes me uncomfortable. It's like being with my father, always being judged.* He knew that in order to win Cindy and her family over, he needed to elevate himself to the social status of the wealthy, a class he's been trying to escape. He heard it in her voice as she described her elegant Thanksgiving dinner served on fine china, crystal goblets, and sterling silverware. She described the family gathering around a long black marble table top with cherrywood French provincial legs in a massive dining room. The wait staff began the parade of food with goose paté and ended with chocolate tortes, pies, and puddings. As Raymond listened, he was thankful for the informality of Walt's home. *I need time to sort this all out.* He tried returning to sleep, but it didn't come. His thoughts were on his future and he hoped it included Cindy.

CHAPTER 18

▼

THE BIG DECISION

The 1937 winter in New York was brutal. Three separate storms brought an accumulation of forty inches of snow with temperatures in the teens. Raymond hardly noticed. He was high on confidence. The first semester was over and his grades received accolades. He reasoned, *I have a good chance in the legal profession, but I need a plan to pursue my aspirations. Nothing is out of reach. I'm ready to meet Cindy's family.* He had come a long way in the last two months. During that time, Raymond had been depressed and not ready to meet Cindy's family. Cindy left for the Bronx angry that he had refused to join her. "I'm just not ready yet," he pleaded to Cindy. She didn't understand his apprehension. Raymond worked a double shift to keep busy while she was gone. When he had free time, he visited his favorite tourist spots. He never tired of the history or art museum. He attended the matinees of Broadway plays such as

the big musical hit *I'd Rather Be Right,* with George M. Cohan.
Afterwards, it was dinner at Derby's. So many times he wanted
to enter a bar for a drink to take away the pain of loneliness.
Out of desperation, he called home. After many attempts, he
realized his family had gone out west for the holiday to visit his
father's brother, Uncle Bob. He thought about contacting Dr.
Debrinski to talk. *I can't; it feels like a step backwards.* One week
away from Cindy felt like an eternity. Walt tried cheering him
up with his English impersonations as he served him dessert.

"I say, old fellow, have a spot of tea with crumpets."

He grinned, but continued to brood. Finally, three days after
New Year's Eve, Raymond received a letter from NYU congrat-
ulating him on his high achievement. He couldn't wait any
longer and called Cindy to tell her of his accomplishment.
When he read the letter, she replied, "I received one too." They
laughed. Their studying together had paid off.

"Cindy, I've decided I'm ready to meet your parents over the
summer. Also, I'm thinking of joining a law firm to complete
my third-year law school requirements. For my second year, I
am pursuing courses in criminal, corporate, and international
law."

"Talk to my father, Raymond. He'll give you guidance."

Raymond knew this would be his last year at Derby's. He
would miss the friendships he had built, but it was time to move
on. *I need exposure to the legal system,* he decided, *and maybe join
a school committee or clerk in the courts. Next fall, I'll look for
recruiters on campus to find a prominent law firm that handles
high profile cases.* His excitement rose. *I have so many plans and*

so much to do to insure my future. I still need classes in legal writing, litigating, and evidence.

It was Monday night and Raymond had finished a hard day at school and work. He needed sleep after a late Saturday night with Cindy. They had eaten an early dinner and enjoyed the opera *La Boheme. I've got to get some sleep tonight,* thought Raymond as he pulled down his bed. Suddenly, the phone rang. He picked up the receiver wondering who was calling this late. *I just spoke to Cindy.* He picked up the receiver and after hearing, "Hello," he was shocked to hear his father's voice at the other end.

"Hi, son. I wanted to call you sooner, but politics takes its toll. How is law school treating you?"

Raymond related his high grades and the letter of achievement.

"I'm proud of you, son."

Raymond choked. "I never thought I'd hear you say those words, Father."

"I called to say I'm running for state representative."

"Did you call to check that your son is no longer a threat and it's safe to further your political career?"

"Why are you always so hostile?"

"I'm sorry, Father. I guess it's out of habit. I'm glad you called. I tried calling you and mom to tell about all the changes in my life, but there is never an answer. Dad, I don't think I can continue my job at Derby's. I need to work at a law firm to get some exposure and maybe volunteer at school to develop contacts. My second year will demand time."

Finally, his father could relate to his son's dilemma. "Schmoozing" was familiar to Mr. Miller and the bloodline to his profession. "No problem, Raymond. You're going in the right direction. I'll foot the bill for everything."

Lastly and hesitantly, he announced there was a love in his life, Cindy Stranton. "I plan to ask her father for her hand in marriage after I receive my law degree. Marriage will come after I land a job at a distinguished firm."

Taken aback by the news, his father was silent momentarily.

"I'm happy for you, son. You're on the path to a successful life. Tell me a little about Cindy and her background."

Normally, that comment would arouse anger in Raymond, but he controlled himself. "Don't worry dad. Cindy comes from old money. Her father is Randall Stranton."

"The famous attorney?"

"That's right."

"Wow! You certainly made a good catch and it can't hurt your career."

Raymond laughed, "You'll never change. Remember, I love her. The rest is pure gravy."

"When the time is right, son, we'll come to meet Cindy and her family. You're maturing and making good choices. I'm proud to call you son."

Raymond couldn't believe his ears. His father had praised him again. *I'm winning the war. Dad is starting to treat me as an equal, a person, a mature adult.* He said his goodbyes and retreated to bed. This time there were no tears, just smiles.

CHAPTER 19

▼

RAYMOND MILLER, JR. (1937-1938)

Farewells were difficult for Raymond. He experienced two significant ones: Leaving home and leaving Rosemont. Now, he was leaving Derby's. Walt insisted on a going-away party.

"I'll be back as a customer. I'm just turning in my apron."

Walt laughed and patted him on the back, saying, "Once you're a big shot attorney, you won't be back."

Raymond never thought in those terms but realized Walt was right.

Cindy was coming in from the Bronx to attend the Saturday gathering. Walt, Midge, Tiffany, Arnold, daytime cook, and a few regular customers were coming. After the party, Raymond promised Cindy he would return with her to the family compound. No more excuses. No backing down. Two weeks before starting their second year in law school, Raymond planned to meet the Stranton family.

The doorbell rang and he knew it was Cindy. He took one last look in the mirror, straightened his tie, grabbed his valise, and ran down the stairs. She stood there looking serene and confident. Her blue-and-white print cotton dress cinched her waistline to mold her petite body. Raymond stared at her beauty and thought how lucky he was to find his sweetheart. I wish I could sweep her in my arms, carry her to my apartment, and make love, but instead he gave her a long hard kiss.

The party was ready to start as Raymond and Cindy walked into Derby's. All the guests arrived and Walt made corned beef sandwiches, coleslaw, and potato salad. Dill pickles and Bravo soda sat on the tables. There was plenty of chatter and good luck wishes to both. Walt made his emotional speech describing Raymond as a good, honest, dependable employee, and said he felt like a son to him. Raymond thought, *It took Walt only a year and a half for me to feel like his son and my father only recognized this after my first year achievement in law school.* Walt brought Raymond up to him and handed him a box.

"This is from all of us and wishing you the best future."

Raymond held back his emotions and gave Walt a hug. He opened the box to find a Parker fountain pen. Walt affirmed, "This is to use when you begin your new role as attorney."

As Cindy and Raymond left Derby's and headed towards the train station for the Bronx, his mind was focused on the week ahead of him. He knew that after staying at Cindy's home, there would be no turning back. He was entering a new life: a life of importance and wealth.

The chauffeur was waiting for them as they exited the train. Cindy introduced him to Ralph. Their ride to the Grand Concourse seemed short, as Cindy told him childhood stories. When they arrived, he glanced out the window to see a grandiose structure: the Stranton Mansion. He tried to act calm and matter-of-fact, as if this was the life he was accustomed to living. His father was well-off, but not on this scale. Cindy introduced him to Matilda, the lady who ruled the roost or gave orders to the other staff. Cindy's parents were still up and welcomed Raymond to their home.

"We'll talk more in the morning," stated Randall and he marched off with his wife, Lucille, to their bedroom suite. Cindy took Raymond around to show him the house and his sleeping quarters.

"My room is down the hall, but don't get any ideas." she playfully teased. Raymond was too nervous over this family visit to have such thoughts. He figured getting an erection was next-to-impossible.

Raymond thought, *at least the family welcomed me with no apprehension. Mr. Stranton asked the standard questions about school and my intent with law. Mrs. Stranton asked about my family, their likes and dislikes. They were impressed when I announced my father's political plans.*

Cindy's brother, Daryl, who practices law in his father's firm, followed his father's direction with questions regarding school and outside interests like sports. Daryl was a star athlete at Notre Dame. Football was his game.

"Your brother probably thought I was dull when I showed no interest in physical activities." Cindy smiled with relief that Raymond wasn't a sports enthusiast.

"Raymond, my high school years were consumed with listening to father and Daryl discuss football. Now, they discuss legal cases. However, when I join the firm, it will change. I'll finally be included in their inner circle of debate."

Raymond detected a little animosity in Cindy's voice. *They're only three years apart, but I sense the competition between them.* Raymond concluded, *if Mr. Stranton offered me a job at his firm, I would decline. It's dangerous to be another competitor between Cindy and Daryl.*

The week passed quickly and Cindy showed him around the Bronx and all the landmarks. He met many of her friends and they all came from old money with the goal of maintaining their position in life. *Could I live in this environment?* He repeated this to himself all week and concluded: If it meant having Cindy, he could.

On the night before departure, Mr. Stranton called him into his office. Raymond sat down in a black leather chair. He offered a cigarette; Raymond declined. He wondered what this tall, thin, self-assured man was going to propose.

"Raymond, I think you know by now my daughter is very fond of you. She tells me you're bright and a high achiever. I could use a person like you in my law firm."

"Mr. Stranton, I love Cindy and when I'm settled in my profession, I will ask for her hand in marriage. However, I think it's best that I seek employment in another firm and prepare for the orals. Too many family members at one firm may not be wise."

Mr. Stranton chuckled, "You have a point there, Raymond. In fact, you have a very good point!" Raymond shook his hand and left the room.

Early the next morning, Raymond found the Strantons in the dining room enjoying their breakfast. He approached them with thanks for a wonderful week.

"Sit down, Raymond," Mrs. Stranton requested. "Have breakfast before Ralph drives you and Cindy to the train station."

Raymond pulled out a tufted gold chair and sat down. Cindy came down the stairs to join him. Raymond knew this make-believe world would end when he returned back to Manhattan. *Cindy retreats to the dormitory. I return to my hovel, but it will feel good to start the second year of law school.*

Raymond met his mentor, Professor Jenkins, in the hall after the first week of classes.

"Professor, can I see you in your classroom at around 3:00 p.m.?" Raymond knew Jenkins was free at that time.

"Sure, Raymond. Is it anything special?"

"I want to discuss doing research for you."

Raymond arrived five minutes early to their meeting, eager to make his proposal.

"Sit down, Raymond." The professor gestured Raymond to a chair.

"I learned you are planning to write a book on criminal cases and could use a researcher. You know that's my specialty. Since I'm no longer working, I can spend more time in the library."

"Is there any other reason, Raymond?"

"It will also look good on my record when the recruiters come this fall. I need an edge over the other students."

"I heard you're on the disciplinary committee. Won't that, plus your studies, take up too much time?"

"I don't think I'll be too busy to watch for students not following the school code. This summer, I took an evidence and legal writing class to be ahead."

Professor Jenkins was amused over Raymond's tenacity. The young man reminded him of himself when he was just starting out.

"Okay, Raymond, we have a deal, but if you get bombarded with work, you'll have to stop."

Raymond shook his hand and thanked him.

"I'll make an appointment next week and we can go over the cases. You won't be sorry," he yelled as he left the room.

Raymond was anxious to meet Cindy at the library and tell her the good news. Cindy looked a little sad as he told her all about the afternoon with Jenkins.

"What's the matter, Cindy? You look unhappy."

"I'm just afraid you'll be so busy, there will be no time for us." Raymond placed his arm around her shoulder: "Cindy, you'll always come first."

"If you came to daddy's firm, Raymond, you wouldn't have to go through all this."

"Cindy, I need to do this on my own. Trust me, it's for the best."

Raymond didn't want to tell her the truth that he thought too many family members in one business can create problems.

It was late fall when the recruiters descended upon the campus looking for the best and brightest students. Raymond had appointments with five firms. They all asked the same questions and were impressed with Raymond's abilities and campus involvement. However, there was one firm which stood out in Raymond's mind: Hutchinson, Tate, and Forster. Mr. Tate was young, in his late thirties, and seemed to have fresh ideas and exuberance. Raymond thought, *I could fit into this environment. I could clerk for a judge this summer, take some extra classes, and start with the firm in the fall. Hopefully, I will receive a letter* of *intent within the next month.* The letter came in two weeks stating that the firm was impressed with Raymond and looked forward to his joining Hutchinson, Tate, and Forster. Raymond was ecstatic and couldn't wait to call Cindy and his father. Cindy was happy because he no longer had to spend extra time interviewing other law firms. There was more time for her. His father was happy because he found a distinguished firm to join, which could be beneficial for his new post of state representative.

CHAPTER 20

▼

THE INFAMOUS CASE

In June, 1938, Raymond finished his second year of law school. It was a hectic but productive year. Raymond called Cindy to let her know of his good fortune.

"Cindy, you won't believe that Professor Jenkin's book is being published and my name is under the acknowledgements for doing the research. My strategy is paying off. My future law firm will be especially impressed. I'm sending a copy of the book to my father."

Raymond wanted to include the name Dr. Debrinski on the list to receive a copy, but didn't mention this to Cindy. To date his secret was protected within the Miller family.

"I received the letter of confirmation from Judge Nolan's office and my clerking will begin in June. I just learned today that Judge Nolan will give the orals on the law exam. Hopefully, if everything goes well, I'll be a full-fledged attorney by 1939."

Outwardly, Cindy exclaimed how pleased she was to hear Raymond so enthralled over his projects and successes. Secretly, however, she felt a little down. Cindy wished other firms had recruited her instead of finding herself sandwiched between her father and brother's law career. Raymond wondered, *is there some apprehension in her voice?* He was so jubilant that he didn't pay much attention.

"I might get involved with international law, Cindy. I've been reading in the newspaper about the turbulence in Europe. My services, as negotiator, might be welcomed." Cindy laughed at his grandiose ideas.

"Get your law degree first, Raymond; then follow your dreams."

Raymond's last year of his curriculum was spent at Hutchinson, Tate & Forster, where he learned the most about law. He studied so many cases that Raymond began to imagine himself in the courtroom as a litigator. When it came to standing in front of Judge Nolan for his exam, he felt at ease. Their relationship had blossomed since his clerking experience last summer. Raymond wasn't intimidated by his power.

In the fall of 1939, Raymond affixed his name plaque on the office door. It read, "Raymond Miller, Jr., Attorney-at-Law." He polished it with the back of his suit sleeve and smiled broadly as he entered the room. Mr. Tate already had cases stacked on his desk. He opened up the first folder to review, when the phone rang. It was Sandra Sloan, Raymond's personal secretary.

"Yes, Miss Sloan."

"There is a Tiffany Maxwell in the waiting room for you and she doesn't have an appointment."

"That's all right. Just send her in."

I wonder what Tiffany from Derby's wants. I hope Walt is okay. As Tiffany entered, Raymond noticed a big bandage wrapped around her right hand.

They gave a quick hug as he asked, "What happened to you?"

He gestured for her to sit down. She sat on his inviting new black leather sofa and started to relate her story.

"The driver delivered three cases of Bravo soda to the restaurant and stacked them in the back room. When I had some spare time, I started placing the bottles in the refrigerator. Boom! A bottle exploded. Glass scattered everywhere. Fragments sliced and diced my hand and arm. Blood was gushing."

Raymond grimaced. "My muscles, tendons, and blood vessels were severed. Lord, it almost cut off my thumb. I went through extensive surgery and I'm still trying to recuperate. I hurt, I'm tired, and I need money. Can I sue Bravo? I can no longer work and hardly use my hand."

Raymond thought about it a while after asking many questions. *This could be the first big case I bring to the firm. Tiffany doesn't have much money, so I can't charge her until we win and collect. If I win this case from Bravo, it could put a feather in my cap. I can make big money and buy Cindy an engagement ring.*

"Tiffany, I want to take the case, but I must confer with Mr. Tate before giving my final answer."

"Raymond, my savings are small and medical bills high. Maybe we can work something out for old times' sake."

"Don't worry Tiffany; we'll take care of the details."

He gave her a peck on the forehead as he showed her out.

"I'll call you with the final decision," he said.

Raymond grabbed a legal pad and proceeded to Tate's office. He knocked on the door hoping Tate was still in.

"Come on in." Raymond entered in a hurry anxious to explain the recent developments.

Tate frowned, "This is a big case for someone just starting in the firm."

"I have confidence I can do it."

"Well, okay, but she'll need to sign an agreement that we receive forty percent of the settlement if you win the case. Also, confer with me on your tactics for pursuing Bravo."

Raymond nodded as he left the room and ran to his office to call Cindy.

"Cindy, I can't believe my luck." He started to unfold the day's events.

"How are you going to approach the case?"

"I know it's tort law, so I'll have to prove negligence. That will be difficult, since I have no proof. How am I going to show the bottle was defective or Bravo had a faulty inspection system or did they deviate from their standards? There isn't a bottle to analyze. All the pieces were swept up and thrown out. I'm not sure, Cindy, but the search may be impossible."

She was silent.

Suddenly, a bell went off in Cindy's head. "Wait a minute, Raymond. Don't try to prove the manufacturer was negligent; infer it. I remember coming across a case, when researching for tort law. I think the company was Premier. I can't remember the specifics, but if you look up the court case, I'm sure the details are there."

"Thanks, Cindy. You're a doll. I'm leaving for the law library now. I'll call you when I'm done and we'll meet for dinner."

"Good luck, Raymond."

The library brought back pleasant memories of the many hours Raymond had spent with Cindy. He found his favorite spot near the card catalog. He looked up tort cases during the thirties and found the 1937 case, *Shirley Dunn v. Premier Bottling Co. of Seattle.* The case was very similar to his and the outcome was in favor of the plaintiff. The court ruled: "The bottler was strictly liable even if it cannot be proven negligent. Imposing strict liability encourages manufacturers to go an extra mile to produce safer products."

That's it, thought Raymond. *That will be my strategy. I'll infer when an accident like Tiffany's occurs, it only occurs because someone is negligent. In this case, it was Bravo. The Premier ruling sets precedence.*

CHAPTER 21

▼

THE TRIAL

After taking Tiffany's deposition about the accident, Raymond made an appointment with the executives at Bravo. Mr. Breecher, the president, and his partner, Mr. Lowe, awaited Raymond's arrival. Their attorney, Mr. Applebaum, sat sternly at Breecher's desk ready for a debate after Raymond presented his case. Raymond asked for one million dollars in damages. Bravo's trio looked stunned and laughed "preposterous." Breecher's round face reddened as he stated, "You'll never prove our company was at fault."

Raymond picked up his briefcase and headed toward the door. With his hand on the knob, he muttered, "I guess I'll see you in court" and left.

It took six months to get a court date and prepare the case. Raymond was nervous. If he won, referrals would follow and his name would become known. Cindy conveyed the message that her father and brother approved of his tenacity and wished him well. Raymond took it as a personal challenge. If he lost the case, they would think him a failure.

Cindy promised Raymond that she'd be in court to hear his opening statement. As she pushed the doors open, Cindy was startled by the roomful of spectators eager to hear testimony against a big corporation versus the working class. Walt came to support Tiffany. Raymond didn't tell his parents of the trial, fearing his father would fly in to observe his performance. He needed all his composure for his first big case. Seeing his father's eyes affixed on him wasn't a challenge he could handle.

"The court will come to order for the case of *Russell v. Bravo Bottling Company of New York,* Judge Nolan presiding."

The courtroom became silent. Raymond stood up and outlined for the jury Bravo's failure to exercise reasonable care.

"I will show what caused the explosion and how it was the obligation of the bottling company to prevent this from happening."

Raymond's first witness was Mr. Johnson, a retired supervisor from Bravo.

"Mr. Johnson, explain to the jury what may have caused the explosion."

"A few things could contribute to the problem. First, the bottle itself may be defective. Secondly, if the bottle is filled with too high a pressure, it could explode."

Raymond felt he was getting his message across of inferring Bravo's negligence and dismissed the witness after several more questions.

Next, he called Tiffany to the stand. She wore a black dress with a white Peter Pan collar and cuffs. Her right hand was wrapped in a high and noticeable bandage. Tiffany looked like a downtrodden employee. She gave testimony as to how the accident occurred and took off the bandages to show her injuries. With sobs and tears rolling down her cheeks, Tiffany described her pain and her inability to earn a living.

After one day of witnesses, the plaintiff rested his case. Bravo called their own expert consultants who testified that there was no way to detect or prove that the bottle was defective or that the company deviated from its careful standards. Bravo's foreman, Mr. Sheppard, testified and gave the company's safety statistics.

The trial lasted three days. Cindy spent so much time at court that her father reminded her of the clients she represented and that they were being overlooked.

"Are you neglecting your clients, Cindy? Doris is getting a lot of calls from clients saying you're not returning their messages."

"I'm sorry, daddy, but Raymond needs my support."

"I hear he's doing great. He can make it on his own."

"I just want to be there for his summation and the verdict. Then I'll give full attention to my cases."

Her father smiled, shook his head, and walked into his office.

Cindy sat in the front row waiting to hear Raymond's closing. He gave the case his best effort and closed with a persuasive summary of Bravo's obligations.

"Ladies and gentlemen of the jury, it was Bravo who acted carelessly in either producing or failing to detect the problem."

Cindy looked at the jury's faces as Raymond finished his summation and felt he won them over. It took the jury only one hour to reach a decision. The verdict was guilty for Bravo and the judgment against the company was over a million dollars. The courtroom audience cheered. Reporters finished their notes and rushed to the press offices. Tiffany hugged Raymond.

"I knew you could do it."

Walt gave Raymond his famous pat on the back and said, "You're the greatest!"

Cindy ran to him, wrapped her arms around his waist and lovingly whispered, "You were brilliant, darling. Now I have to get back to work."

When Raymond approached his office, there were cheers from the employees and a handshake from Mr. Tate.

"You did a good job, Raymond. I'm glad you selected our firm. If we see a significant increase in business due to your victory, the reward will be in your paycheck."

Raymond was elated. He thought, *In one day I earned the respect of my peers and was compensated with enough money to ask Cindy for her hand in marriage. I must speak to Mr. Stranton.*

The next day, Mr. Miller, Sr., was in his office when the phone rang.

"Ray, did you read the *Times* this morning?"

"No, dear, I haven't had a chance. I was going to read it at lunch."

"Well, look at the front page."

Mr. Miller went out to the receptionist and asked for the newspaper.

"What could be so important that Margaret called all excited?" He grabbed the paper and on the front page read, "Young attorney wins Bravo case."

When he saw his son's name, he couldn't believe it. He ran to the phone. "Margaret, it's our Raymond. He made it big and didn't even call to tell us."

Immediately, Miller called his son at work. The line was continuously busy. Finally after an hour, a feminine voice answered,

"Raymond Miller, Jr's office. How may I help you?"

"This is Mr. Miller's father. Is he in?"

"One moment, sir."

"Hi, Dad. I wanted to call before the papers hit the streets, but the phone won't stop ringing."

"I know, son. I've been calling ever since I read the front page. Why didn't you tell us about your high profile trial? Coming to New York to see you in action deserved top priority."

"I wanted to surprise you and Mom if I won."

Raymond's true feelings, fear of losing, were kept silent.

"I hope you're proud of my accomplishment."

"We're both proud of you. You've become the son we always wanted."

"Dad, now that my position at the firm is secure and my financial potential strong, I'm going to ask Cindy to marry me. I'm meeting with Mr. Stranton tomorrow to obtain his approval. Once it's official, I want you and mom to come to New York and meet Cindy and her family. And dad, one day I'm going to bring Cindy to Detroit. Since my name is plastered over the newspapers, you don't need to be paranoid anymore. I think it's safe to return home."

Mr. Miller totally ignored what Raymond just said to him. Instead, he said, "Good-luck son. Keep in touch."

Detective Pierce sat at his desk with a cup of coffee and a newspaper.

"Well, I'll be darned. Hey, McQuire, listen to this: 'Young attorney wins Bravo case.' Who do you think the attorney is?"

"Beats me."

"The disappearing Raymond Miller, Jr. He makes a quick getaway from Detroit and five years later ends up in New York City on the front page of the *Times*."

"Looks like he made a name for himself in spite of his drinking problem," replied McQuire.

"Yeah. Well I'm not quite convinced. I think I'll follow his career for a while. Maybe he'll slip up," announced Pierce.

Down the block at the Detroit News Building, Ron Spector, the reporter on the Rebecca Abrom case, read the headlines, and came to the same conclusion. *I wonder if our boy is hiding any information regarding an old case.*

CHAPTER 22

▼

NERVOUS BREAKDOWN

Only one day had passed since Nate rode the ambulance with Becky tied to a stretcher and repeating out of control, "She's not dead; you lied."

Nate worked all night, but couldn't go home before seeing his wife. He walked in her room at Receiving's psychiatric ward and saw her strapped to a chair staring out at space.

"Becky, it's me; Nate. How are you doing?"

No response. Alarmed, he went to find Dr. Shapiro.

"I'm sorry; the doctor is seeing patients," stated the secretary at the nurses' station. "Can you make an appointment?"

"When is he free?"

"Lunch is in an hour. He can see you at noon."

"Fine. I'll grab something to eat and return."

Nate was exhausted after the last forty-eight hours of events. He walked to the corner coffee shop to try and eat some eggs.

Lately, his stomach felt heavy with pressure above his navel. When he burped after eating, it left an acid taste. The other day he noticed some blood in his stool, but dismissed it as hemorrhoids. *I can't get sick. I need to take care of Becky.* He glanced at his watch. *I better start back. I don't want to miss the doctor.* As soon as he arrived on the ninth floor and registered, the nurse asked him to follow her. She took him into Dr. Shapiro's small paneled office with a stack of papers piled on his desk. Books lined the shelves. *I wonder how he can find anything under that mess*, thought Nate. Dr. Shapiro motioned for Nate to have a seat and came around from his desk to shake his hand. The doctor was short and slight. His thick black hair was parted to one side. He spoke softly and displayed a slow, patient demeanor.

"Dr. Shapiro, must my wife be strapped to her chair? She's not moving or speaking."

"Now that she's sedated, we can take the straitjacket off."

Nate shook his head in frustration, as he tried to explain his current circumstances.

"I can't believe this is happening. Our life was finally coming out of disarray since her accident."

"Mr. Abrom, your wife was told unexpected horrifying news by phone from a stranger. She went into shock, and the affect landed in the weakest part of her body, her legs."

"Doctor, will Becky ever walk again?"

"I believe so, once we treat her shock and depression."

"Our family is in mourning. Her sister is being buried tomorrow, then Shiva begins for seven days. I know Becky can't attend. Her younger brother, Jake, just arrived home from the army. What a reception. One sister dead and one sister in a mental hospital. What can I do to get my wife home?"

"Mr. Abrom, Rebecca received one session of psychoanalysis with no response. I would like to try electroshock therapy to see if I can reach her faster."

"What kind of treatment is that?"

"'The official name is Electroconvulsive Therapy or ECT. Electrodes will be placed on Rebecca's temples and her brain is briefly stimulated with electricity resulting in a brief seizure. This treatment causes changes in the chemistry of the brain that are beneficial to the patient.'"

"I don't know. That sounds dangerous to me. Is it painful?"

"Mr. Abrom, watching your wife is painful. If we can't get her to respond to therapy, she will be here a long time."

"Doctor, I don't have that kind of money. I have a little saved, but not for a long hospital stay and I won't put her into a state mental asylum. Go ahead and try the shock treatment."

"It's worth a try," reassured Shapiro. "Although, no guarantees."

"When will you try the first one?"

"Maybe in a day or two. I'll let you know when it's scheduled."

Nate shook hands again with the doctor and left. He went to say goodbye to Becky, but found it fruitless.

As he left the hospital, he felt the energy draining from his body. His lower back ached from standing on his feet all night baking. He quickly crossed Woodward Avenue to catch the bus. Once aboard, he tried keeping his eyes open. They kept fluttering closed with the motion of the vehicle. He felt that repeated burning feeling in the pit of his stomach. *It must be nerves*, he thought, as he rehashed Becky's mental status. *I wonder if letting the doctors fool around with her brain is wise? What if shock treatment does damage? Dr. Shapiro didn't address those issues. It can't be worse then she is now—or could it?* Nate saw his stop and rang the buzzer.

As he stepped down, he looked at his watch. It read two o'clock. *I have two hours before the girls come home from school. What do I tell them?* When Nate reached home, he quickly took his pants off and tried to nap. A knock at the door woke him up. He put his pants back on to answer it. Mary stood in the doorway with a tray of chicken, roast potatoes, and salad for their dinner.

"It is so nice of you to think of us."

"I know you can use some help, Nate. How is Becky?"

"Not so good," he said, as he repeated the doctor's diagnosis and proposed treatment.

Mary reassured him that Becky would be home soon and offered her services, if needed. As he closed the door, he thought, *How lucky we are to have the Wilburs upstairs. Mary brings down food and watches Dena. Rena is old enough to help around the house, but supervision is needed to keep Rena and Dena from fighting. I wonder why those two can't get along better.* Nate took his pants off again and finally fell asleep. It wasn't long before he heard noises at the side door and feet running up six steps to their flat. The girls looked for their father, hoping he could answer questions about their mother. It frightened them to see her being carried out in a stretcher. The girls ran into the bedroom together.

"What happened to mom?" "When is she coming home?" they both asked simultaneously.

Dena added, "We need her to take care of us."

"I can take care of myself," retorted Rena in a huff, "and besides you have Aunt Mary."

"Yeah, but it's not the same."

Dena spoke sadly, afraid that the secret hidden in her head would be revealed. Nate got out of bed after a short nap.

"Come on, girls, let's go tackle the laundry. I don't know when your mother is coming home and we need clean clothes."

Everyone marched to the basement.

"I hate going down there," complained Rena. "It feels damp and there are spiders."

"I'm afraid of the wringer washer. My fingers can get caught in the rollers," added Dena.

"Quit complaining. If we all have a job, the washing will go faster. I'll put the clothes in the washer and the wringer. Dena, you rinse them in the tubs. Rena, you hang them on the line. When we're done, we'll go up, have ice cream, and discuss a schedule while mommy is in the hospital. Rena, since you are the oldest, you will be responsible for simple meals. Aunt Mary can't always cook. I will try to be home for dinner."

"Sometimes Uncle Jake has dinner with us and tells us jokes. He's funny," laughed Dena.

"We can't count on Uncle Jake every night. He lives here until he can save some money and have his own place, but he has his own life."

Dena questioned, "Why doesn't he live with his father and Bubbie Bertha?"

"Remember, they don't talk to us," quipped Rena. "If it wasn't for Aunt Lilly's funeral, we wouldn't have seen them."

"Why?" Dena was persistent in getting the facts.

"That story is for another time," answered Nate.

He proceeded to lay out a schedule for the girls.

"I expect both you girls to come home from school and start your homework. Dena keeps the bathroom clean and dusts the furniture. Rena makes the dinner and vacuums the carpeting. Both of you do the dishes and keep your bedroom clean. Even when mommy comes home, she will need your help."

Dena asked, "Is mommy sick?"

"Sick in the head," answered Rena.

"That's enough," retorted Nate. "Now let's get ready for bed."

Three days passed before Nate received the phone call from Dr. Shapiro stating Becky's first treatment would begin tomorrow.

"Mr. Abrom, I tried therapy and it's not working, I think we have no choice but to try shock."

"Okay, doctor. Do you want me there?"

"You need to sign a permission form before we can proceed."

"I'll be there right after work."

Nate felt that sharp pain in his stomach again as he hung up the phone. He considered; *what if something goes wrong and Becky stays withdrawn. I might lose her forever.*

Nate felt his heart palpitate as he rushed to reach Becky before the orderly took her for treatment. The gurney rolled towards the room with the sign, "Keep Out." Becky's body remained still with straps wrapped around her. Nate arrived just in time to grab her hand and give it a squeeze. "Good luck, honey."

Becky turned her head and seemed sedated. The door opened and with the squeak of the wheels, she was pushed forward and disappeared from sight. He walked away, head down, shoulders drooped, and smelling defeat in the air. He felt the weight of the family's future resting on his decision.

A chill rippled down Becky's body as she grimaced from the bright lights. Suddenly a look of fear erupted in her eyes. Nurse Henning reassured her.

"Now, sweetie, don't be frightened. I'll be here by your side. I'm just placing electrodes on your temples. They'll feel like cold knobs hugging the skin."

Becky thought it felt like a vise holding her head in place. She tried to get up and cry out, but her body felt like lead and her voice dried up. The orderly placed a rubber tube between her teeth to prevent Becky from biting her tongue. She felt a surge of current blast through her head. Her body jerked and she fell into a stupor.

Becky went through this procedure two more times before Dr. Shapiro started to see progress. The healing process was far from over. However, Nate needed to bring her home. He hired a nurse for less then the cost of her stay in the ward. Before they left the hospital, Dr. Shapiro reaffirmed that Becky needed rest and psychoanalysis once a week.

"It appears that Becky's accumulation of tragedies since age twelve clashes with her mental and internal capabilities to handle any more sadness."

"Dr. Shapiro, as long as I can make payments, Becky will keep her appointments."

As they rode the bus home, Nate thought about the mounting medical expenses. He took the flyer out of his pocket that he had grabbed off the table in Dr. Shapiro's office. It read "Blue Cross Insurance Plan." He remembered someone at work discussing it with his boss. It stated that for a flat monthly fee, the company would pay hospital bills and physician fees. He glanced at his wife with her head resting on the window sill and knew his medical expenses would be ongoing. He knew Becky's setback would wipe out the money saved from the butcher business. *I need to start over, but how many times can I do this. I'll discuss this idea with Becky once she's better and see if our budget can handle the cost.*

Becky's spirits improved once she returned home and saw the girls had kept her house in order. She tried to get back to a routine; however, the nurse insisted on rest. Dena found her mother in bed when she came home from school and crawled in with her. Dena, at six, felt secure cuddled up to her warm body. On weekends, people were always visiting and Rena and Dena hated the intrusion. They never divulged their opinion in fear of upsetting their mother.

Within a month, Becky discharged the nurse. She needed to get back to keeping up the house in her fashion. She resumed weekly visits with Dr. Shapiro in an attempt to connect how her feelings of guilt from not fulfilling Bertha's demands, and feelings of abandonment over the loss of her mother and siblings were mentally and physically crippling her. However, Becky found relief not in the therapy, but from shopping. This was the catalyst that filled her holes of emptiness. She couldn't buy enough. She kept the girls in new clothes from Baker's Department Store, along with porcelain blue and pink birds for the dining room table and a mink coat from Wrubel and Kosin. The bills came in fast and furious. Nate didn't know how to confront her. If he did, she always responded, "I don't receive much enjoyment from life, because of my pain, so instead of spending money on trips and entertainment, I buy a few things."

Nate treated Becky like a china doll. He reasoned, *If I put too much pressure on her, she might have another breakdown.* Besides, it wasn't his nature to be confrontational. Out of fear of going bankrupt or taking on more jobs, Nate called Dr. Shapiro and explained his problem. The doctor realized he needed to take another approach in handling his patient.

Their sessions focused on how it wasn't Becky's fault that her mother died. Her accident wasn't the punishment. Becky felt robbed of her childhood and guilty for resenting Bertha.

"What made Bertha so mad at me that she convinced her family I am the enemy? I never see my half-siblings. They hate me. She feeds their minds with poisonous lies and they believe her. Am I such a bad person?"

It took the psychiatrist and Becky about a year to rid her mind of the demons that resided in her head and mend the pieces of her broken heart. Eventually, the excessive shopping stopped and she returned to the role of prudent mother and wife.

CHAPTER 23

▼

THE RAPE

Home from school on a balmy fall day, Dena went looking next door for her best friend, Bonnie, to play jacks outside on their front porch. The two girls were inseparable. Bonnie's sister explained to Dena that Bonnie and her mother went shopping. *Now I have no one to play with*, thought Dena. *What shall I do? I know; I'll go look for Aunt Mary and see what she's doing. Maybe she's baking those great apple pies.*

Dena ran upstairs and knocked on the door hoping to find Aunt Mary with her apron on, busy in the kitchen. Instead, a voice called, "Come in."

Dena opened the door and walked in to find Fred Wilbur in his sleeveless white undershirt, whiskers around his face, relaxing in his lounger.

"Hi," greeted Dena. "I came to visit with Aunt Mary."

"She went to an early show with her sister and to dinner. They won't be back until late. Are you looking for something to do?"

Dena nodded her head, "yes."

"I have a good game we can play, but we need to go to the bedroom."

Dena wondered; *What could it be? Maybe hide and seek.* Fred took Dena's hand and they walked down the hallway. He placed her on their high double bed on top of the white Chantilly lace bedspread. Then, he gently pulled down her jeans and panties. The bedspread felt prickly under her bottom. Dena thought this was an odd game, but at age seven she trusted him. He tenderly slid his finger in the opening of Dena's private part, only known to her as *pee pee*, and slid it up and down. He felt his penis grow. He unzipped his pants and took out his member, placing it inside her womb of innocence. He moved back and forth, making sure he didn't go too far and cause pain. Dena was getting restless and wanted to get up. He frightened her as she looked at his face and saw those glaring eyes and felt his hot, smelly, stale, tobacco breath. He quickly took his organ out of her and felt the wetness penetrate his hand.

"Dena, this is our little game and if you tell anyone, you won't be able to visit Aunt Mary again."

He pulled up her underpants and jeans. She jumped off the bed anxious to get out of there as fast as possible.

"I won't tell anyone, Mr. Wilbur, because I want to see Aunt Mary."

"You promise?"

"I promise."

As Dena ran downstairs, she thought, *I won't tell mother about this. She might not like it and will get upset.*

Dena avoided going upstairs, unless she called to see if Aunt Mary was there. Her mother taught her how to dial the number in case of an emergency. Once, she called and Mr. Wilbur answered.

"Sure. Come up, Dena. Aunt Mary would love to see you."

When she arrived, he was alone and they played the same game. This time, she knew it was wrong. *I'm too scared to tell anyone. I want to cry out, Mom, do you know what happened in the bedroom of the upper flat? I can't. Too many people will be mad at me. Telling mother my story may put her back into the hospital. I can't take that chance. I will keep the secret to myself and pretend it never happened.*

Becky couldn't understand why Dena was seeing less and less of their neighbor. When she questioned Dena, the response was, "I'm too busy playing with Bonnie," or, "I'd rather play by myself."

Becky stopped asking Dena, as she sensed it upset her. *Maybe she's just growing up and doesn't need to be with Aunt Mary as much,* concluded Becky.

CHAPTER 24

▼

DENA (1945-1951)

Through the living room window, Dena watched the snow come down in large flakes. *Christmas and Hanukkah are my favorite time of year*, she reminisced. "I find the season a joyous time. I can't wait to go upstairs and help the Wilburs decorate their tree," she said to her mother as she twirled around the room. Dena was all excited because presents were exchanged on Christmas Eve and she always received a gift from the Wilburs. Aunt Mary served eggnog, fruitcake, sugar cookies, and her famous apple pie. Dena's mouth was watering and her mother laughed to watch her gaiety.

The part of the holiday Dena liked best was going to J.L. Hudson's Department Store to view their decorations and displays, see Santa, and have lunch in the Hudson's café.

"I know at age five I'm too old to sit on Santa's lap, but mommy, I still have the holiday spirit. Remember last year daddy took me to the Thanksgiving parade. I was thrilled when Santa showed up in his sled and received the key to the city. He confirmed the beginning of the festive holiday season and I believed Hudson's Santa was the true one. It sure was windy in downtown Detroit that year. When daddy and I got off the Woodward streetcar, the wind whipped off his hat. I laughed as he went chasing it. He didn't see the humor at first, but watching me giggle gave him a good chuckle."

What made Hanukkah special to the girls? The gifts were appreciated, lighting the candles each night for eight days was meaningful, the games were fun, but Dena described her mother's potato pancakes, called Latkes, as the best. Becky grated the potatoes and onions by hand, mixed in egg and matzo meal and fried them until golden brown. Dena described them as "scrumptious."

Becky participated in the festivities by planning their Saturday trip downtown. "Dena, do you have your white fur muff? We're going to meet Aunt Mary's sister, Dottie, for lunch after visiting Hudson's holiday displays."

"Yes," She yelled. "I don't want to wear this silly hat."

"You must; it matches your coat and leggings and, besides, it's very cold outside."

Becky wore a brown cloth coat with fox collar, brown gloves, and brown felt hat. A large feather floated around the brim. Looking at the feather made Dena smile. She thought, *That feather looks like it came from a Thanksgiving turkey before being stripped clean.* The Abrom family looked like they belonged to high society as they left for downtown. *Funny, we played the role of the wealthy, but I knew there wasn't much money to spend*, Dena concluded. Sometimes, even fifty cents for Rena and me to go to the Dexter movie show with friends was too much. Mother consoled us by saying "Maybe next week." *What confused me was how mother kept buying clothes and items for the house if money was scarce.*

"I don't need another skirt, blouse, sweater or dress," Dena told her mother when they went shopping at Hudson's, but Becky managed to pick something out for her to try on. Dena knew father worked hard and sometimes had two jobs to keep the bills from piling up. She complained to herself, *Why does mother spend so much, while daddy works so hard? Why doesn't he put his foot down and tell her to stop? I think daddy is frightened to say no. He's afraid she might have a setback and return to the hospital.* Occasionally, Nate asked, "Did you need it, Becky?" She'd say, "It was old and needed replacing, or I wanted us to look nice, not shabby."

Mother's possessions always looked brand-new. She brushed, cleaned, washed, and ironed her clothes. Then, she placed them in garment bags to protect them from dust and any bugs. Furniture was covered in plastic. Nothing ever looked old or used. If an item didn't meet her standards, it was given away. Nate never disputed her philosophy. If Dena complained about her mother's extravagance, he'd say, "Don't upset your mother."

Dena thought, *What did that mean? She was always upset over something. She yelled about the house not being clean enough, but to me it was spotless. My sister and I had cleaning jobs. We were taught how to clean the bathroom properly. That was my job. I had*

to scrub the tile, bathtub, toilet bowel top and bottom and get into
the corners of the floor. After cleaning the sink, I had to make sure
the chrome faucets were shined.

Becky always criticized the way Rena did her job.

"I can tell you don't care how you clean," she said.

Dena was bothered by her mother always yelling at Rena over
something.

Becky worried about so much that you wondered when she
had time to sleep. Nate called her a worry wart. Dena believed
she'd get warts from worrying so much. During the forties, their
parents worried about them contracting polio. Their mother's
worst fear was that if one of her girls became ill with the crippling disease and couldn't breathe, one might need to be placed
in an iron lung for respiratory treatment. Becky's image of her
being crippled after the accident made her paranoid over polio.
The vision of one of her children needing to walk with crutches
overwhelmed her. Summertime increased the risk of getting the
disease, so Becky had rules to follow: Play outside until lunch,
come inside to bathe, change clothes, and sit on the front porch
playing quietly or in the house until the heat of the day was
over. Camp was out of the question, a breeding ground for the
polio goblins to attack kids. Dena wondered if lack of funds was
the real reason for no camp and her mother was too proud to
ask for help. Becky always reported the dangers of any sport the
girls wanted to do. Dena wanted to go swimming with friends
in the Rouge Park pool. Before leaving the house, her mother
read the statistics of how many children drowned in pools. At
night, after her father went to work, all windows were shut with

safety locks in place. *It didn't matter if we died from heat,* Dena recalled. *It was better than being burglarized.*

One day, she asked her mother, "Why are you scared over everything?"

"I couldn't endure one more ounce of pain in my life."

That's when she realized being raised by someone handicapped wasn't easy, because of all their built-in fears.

Dena remembered that the day after school let out for the summer, she rode her bike down the driveway and fell. She ran inside bleeding and crying hysterically, and her mother took a look at her arm swelling and felt nauseous and dizzy. She sat down before passing out. The neighbors came running over to tend to Becky and forgot about Dena.

"Hey there, someone; maybe my arm is broken," she called out but realized her mother needed the attention. Becky was the victim and no one was taking that role away from her. Finally, Nate came to her aid. He moved her arm up, down, around, and was satisfied that no bones were broken. Ice packs were used and, within a few days, Dena's arm returned to its normal size.

Often, Dena lingered in bed thinking: *What would mom be like if she wasn't always ailing? Would her legs be shapely with no scars or limp? Would she drive and take us places? Now, if she didn't want to go or do something, it was due to her pain. No vacations, because she couldn't walk the distance. A wheelchair was forbidden. It didn't matter if my father needed to get away. It was more important that he worked to keep the income flowing. No renting a cottage like so many friends; it was too much work to pack, lug food, and set up a household for a week.* Pain became Becky's usual excuse to stay home. Having no money just reinforced it.

Rena and Dena learned to adapt to family dynamics, although they were tired of people looking at their mother's disability and asking, "What happened to your mother?" They noticed the red, scaly, inflamed skin covering the dented leg. They didn't want to repeat the accident story, but knew it was rude to ignore people's questions. Dena dreamt of having a mother not so high-strung or angry. Then she felt guilty. *It wasn't her fault. At least, I have a mother.* She remembered hearing her mother's stories over and over again. Becky's mother's death, her brother's death, her mean step-mother, the accident, her sister's death, her breakdown. Dena felt, at twelve, she'd never live past twenty. *I'm doomed to die young.*

Of course, there were good times such as the excitement of watching her mother preparing for holiday dinner, inviting company for the occasion, and serving in the dining room. "Tonight, Rena and I are not sitting at the tiny two-person table in the kitchen," Dena rejoiced. Every ounce of Becky's strength was used to prepare the Passover meals for the holiday the Jews celebrated, which represented the exodus from Egyptian slavery. Nate brought up boxes from the basement filled with special Passover dishes. Becky cleaned her cupboards before placing all the items away. She filled the shelves with special kosher foods for the eight-day holiday and gave the non-Passover items away to the Wilburs.

Baking began a week in advance and cakes were stored. Becky prepared three different kinds of gelfite fish, soup, and matzo balls, some filled with meat. The smell of chicken and beef brisket roasting left an intoxicating aroma. Becky's chopped liver, made with fried onions and schmaltz (chicken fat), was her specialty. The house carried a scent of celebration. However, all the work kept their mother in bed for days after the holiday. The pain made her immobile. The girls ran the household until Becky was on her feet again.

For all the yelling and complaining their mother did, their father was the calming force behind the family. He had the patience of a saint. Dena couldn't wait to see him come home from work. In fact, on weekends, if Bonnie and Dena were playing outside and saw Nate coming from the bus stop, they would race toward him to see who could get the first hug. Dena wanted the hugs. She didn't want to share him with anyone. As they argued who reached her dad first, he'd pull out two butterfly rolls from his jacket, as a peace offering. This favorite treat was made with cinnamon and raisins, and baked fresh each morning. They each took one and forgot about the dispute. "Let's play restaurant, Bonnie. We can use the rolls as our food order." Dena ran inside to bring out her plastic dishes and silverware. They played for hours enjoying the rich buttery taste.

Nate was tired from his night shift, but never showed it or complained. He was ready to listen to complaints, understand the family frustrations, and play card games with the girls. Dena remembered the trip to Greenfield Village and how tired she and her sister were after taking three buses to get to Dearborn from Monterey Street and returning home late. Her father took it as part of the adventure. When mother had a chore or job for him to do, he never said no. He just did it. Nothing was too much for Becky or his girls.

Leisure time was in short supply for Nate. Occasionally, he and Becky went out to eat or to a show with friends or invited couples to their house to play cards, but the one thing he took time out for was his "victory garden." Planting "victory gardens" began in 1944, as part of the war effort to conserve. Community residents shared space on vacant land allocated by the city. The garden increased their vegetable supply and cost less then store prices. Some of the seeds ordered from the Victory Garden Company were green beans, carrots, cucumbers, and tomatoes. By 1946, its popularity had decreased. Nate still maintained his garden and brought Dena along to help. Working with his hands was a talent that repeatedly showed up in his early drawings, cake decorating, and gardening. Working outside was exhilarating for him, after leaning over a hot oven all night. Once a week, they'd walk the six blocks to their patch of glory. Dena helped weed with her shovel and picked the crops. "Don't pick the green ones," daddy ordered. She learned fast which tomatoes were ripe and juicy.

Dena talked to herself constantly at home. "Dotdee, do this. Dotdee, let's play. Dotdee, what do you think?" Becky worried about her daughter's imaginary friend and thought maybe she had one because she wasn't close to her sister and used "Dotdee" as a substitute. Dena and Rena were so different. Dena was happy-go-lucky and had many friends, while Rena was quiet and had only two friends. It hurt Becky to see them distant. Their tastes were different. Rena picked at her food, but loved desserts. Dena ate all her food. Rena was tall and thin. Dena was chubby with long curls. Sometimes on a rainy or snowy day, the girls stayed home and played Monopoly or Canasta. Dena told her mother, "I want a sister to do fun sister things like putting on makeup or doing our hair. Rena has no interest. Bonnie's sister is totally different."

This kind of talk depressed Becky, but Dena kept on talking. "When I go next door, her sister, Annette, models her clothes for us, shows us how to apply makeup, and jokes with us. I'm jealous."

Becky blamed herself for their seven-year difference and not being close. *If I didn't have the accident, I'd have more children and ones closer in age.* The day came when Becky's mind was put to ease when her girlfriend, Sally, told her to stop worrying about Dena's "Dotdee." "I read it was a sign of brilliance to have an imaginary friend." "Dotdee" left the household when Dena entered first grade.

When Dena was in elementary school, a crisis happened in the Abrom family and it had nothing to do with Becky's health. For the second time in their marriage, Nate became ill. Becky kept telling her husband to see a doctor. "I can tell you're weak and you keep taking anti-acid tablets. Something is wrong." Finally, he went to Doctor Lossman's office. Tests were done and the doctor found he had a bleeding ulcer. Nate refused surgery. "I can't miss work, Becky," he said.

"Dr. Lossman said you're going to pass out one day from losing too much blood. So if you don't take care of it, he resigns from being your doctor."

Nate went into surgery within a week. He needed six pints of blood before they could operate. Becky said, "There was only one other time your father missed work. It was when we were first married and his appendix was about to burst. The workers at Sanders rushed him to emergency."

"Girls, it seems your father worries about all of us, but when it comes to his health, he uses crisis management."

CHAPTER 25

▼

RENA (1952-1955)

With exuberance, teary eyes, and joy in their heart, Becky and Nate watched Rena walk across the stage to receive her diploma from Central High School in Detroit. Becky gave a sigh of relief. "I thought I'd never see this day," she whispered to Nate. She knew she yelled at Rena too much in regard to her grades. She remembered Rena's teacher, Mrs. Fagen, describing her as being distractible and a daydreamer in class. Becky thought about the day she went berserk after catching Rena trying to change her grade from a "D" to a "B" on her report card. Becky screamed, "You idiot, do you think you can fool me?" She slapped the pen out of her hand. Rena cowered in her room feeling ashamed and desperate. Becky shuddered as she remembered all the arguments with Rena. Becky's philosophy: If you yell and criticize someone enough that person would try harder to change. She wanted Rena to change. Becky's father and step-mother yelled at her and she did her best to please them.

Rena came down the aisle of the auditorium thinking: *I fooled them all and graduated with my 1952 class. It was hard, because I couldn't concentrate in school and hated studying. Being shy and not speaking up didn't mean I was stupid. I was the fastest typist in typing class. My mom was disappointed in me, and in her eyes there wasn't much I could to please her. After enough criticism, one begins to feel useless.*

Her parents greeted her after the graduation ceremony, hugged her, and said, "We are so proud of you, Rena." She shrugged her shoulders, not believing her mother. She knew her father loved her. He always showed kindness. However, she doubted her parents' affection since the time eleven years ago when they brought home from the hospital a little bundle and introduced Rena to her new sister. Everyone made a big fuss over the baby and, growing up, she did very little wrong. Rena felt there was no longer a place for her in the family. She hated her tall lanky body and felt awkward in trying to do sports like the other girls in gym class. She thought most of the kids made fun of her, so she kept to herself, but finally, in high school, she meet two girls she liked and invited them over the house. Rena was embarrassed when her mother hollered because they left fingerprints on the refrigerator door and the house was messy. That was the last time Rena invited them over.

Becky needed Rena's help while raising Dena and gave her responsibility at an early age. She was told what to do and the right way to do it. Rena rode her bike to the corner store and brought back groceries in her basket. She tried to be a good babysitter when her mother needed to do chores, but Rena never got the recognition needed to build her self-esteem.

Rena never understood the relationship with her mother's relatives. Sometimes they talked and got together and other times they were forbidden to mention their names. Rena recalled going to Bubbie Bertha's house in grade school to watch her cook or play with her uncles and aunt. *I liked being part of that family, but mother said Bubbie Bertha was mean to me when I was little and didn't want me visiting alone. I think mother was jealous that I behaved better at their house than at home.*

Job hunting was Rena's next challenge. On the Sunday after graduation, Rena rushed to read the classified section of the *Detroit Times*. She combed the columns until she came upon an ad that read: "Typist wanted: Must type at least eighty words per minute." She placed a check-mark next to the ad. *That's easy,* Rena thought. *I can type ninety words per minute. I'm applying for the job on Monday.* When she received a call back the day after her interview, she jumped for joy. "Mother, I was hired at the Mills Paint Company for $35 a week and I start next Monday." She felt important to be part of the work force and earn a salary. She knew she must pay her mother $5 per week for room and board. *I have big plans for my paycheck. First, I'll open a savings account at American Savings Bank and put away money for my big dream, a trip to New York. Secondly, I'll buy a few new clothes, and a suitcase for the trip.* She asked her friend, Sylvia, to go to New York with her, but she didn't want to spend the money. Rena didn't know if she had the nerve to go by herself. Dena kept saying, "Be brave and go yourself." Becky said, "Nice single girls shouldn't go to a big city alone; too many things can happen." *She always worries and scares me to death. I don't know what to do.* Rena felt confused. *I might surprise everyone and just leave. Maybe I'll go with a tour group and meet people that way.*

After working three years at Mills, Rena was promoted from typist to operating the billing machine. A raise that went with the promotion enabled her to save enough money for her trip. Rena's dream came true at age twenty-two. She gained enough confidence to go alone on a tour to New York in May, 1955. Before leaving, Dena begged her sister to bring her back a cashmere sweater. "Please, please. All the popular girls in Durfee wear them." Dena knew the cost prohibited her parents from indulging her and she would never ask. However, she knew Rena had money, but spending it on an expensive sweater for her was questionable.

Rena came back from her vacation a new person, more independent from being on her own and confident enough to take another trip alone, maybe to California. She couldn't stop talking about the highlights of her trip: Broadway plays, sightseeing, and shopping. She walked miles to see the popular sights like the Empire State Building and the Statue of Liberty. She looked in the windows of the expensive shops on Fifth Avenue, but did most of her buying at Macy's Department Store. The subway took her to lower Broadway, where she spent time on Delancy Street. Storekeepers displayed their wares on tables outside their shops piled high with bargains. They peddled their purses, shoes, clothes, and sundry items to people passing by.

She joined the shoppers and hovered over the merchandise looking for the best buys. Even Leonard's Delicatessen had the dill pickles outside in wooden barrels. Forty-Second Street and Broadway was glitzy with all the lights shining bright at night. Her favorite play was *Damn Yankees*. She didn't miss the1955 big Broadway hit, *The Seven Year Itch*.

After filling her family in with all the details, Rena handed her sister a Macy's bag. Dena couldn't believe it. *She bought me a present. Could it be what I ordered?* She was shaking and couldn't get the bag opened fast enough. She put her hand in and pulled out a beautiful white Robert Altman cashmere sweater. Dena couldn't stop thanking her. "I can't believe you listened to my needs and cared! What a great big sister!"

CHAPTER 26

▼

THE ENGAGEMENT

Raymond kept glancing at the time as he fidgeted with his watchband. He waited in a booth at the Stork Club for Mr. Stranton. Five more minutes until he was due to arrive for their lunch meeting. Raymond kept replaying his thoughts: *What if he refuses my request for his daughter's hand in marriage? Will he accept me into the prominent Stranton family? If he knew my past, I think he would laugh in my face. But he can't trace my background. Dad and I covered our bases. The Detroit police have no proof of a case against me. Even our car was destroyed. Rosemont won't divulge my records nor acknowledge that I was there. So why am I so anxious and worked up? Just relax.*

Finally, Stranton entered the restaurant and the hostess brought him to the table. Raymond got up to shake his hand. "Sit down, sit down, my boy. I'm sorry I'm late, but I had to take a long distance call regarding the Brewster case."

"Do you mean the murder case that you and Cindy are working on?"

"Yes. We think Mr. Brewster was framed for the murder of his business partner."

Raymond inquired, "Do you have proof of that?"

"That's what the call was about. We'll have proof before the preliminary hearing."

"Well, good luck!"

"We'll make it big if we win this case. It smells of racial overtones. There are not many Caucasian and Negro business partners and when the white one shows up dead, it raises a lot of controversy. I must commend you, Raymond, on winning the Bravo case. You did a fine job. In fact, any time you decide to change law firms, we have an opening."

Raymond laughed, "I appreciate that, Mr. Stranton; however, I asked to meet with you for a different reason. First, let's have some lunch."

They both settled on the house specialty, filet mignon. Throughout the meal, Raymond's stomach churned from nervousness. When Stranton finished his coffee, he heard Raymond clear his throat and then sensed that he was ready to reveal the real reason for their meeting.

"I know I have a long way to go in my career with regard to achievements and financial success, but the Bravo case was just the beginning. I'm still learning and growing and would like Cindy to be part of my life. Mr. Stranton, I love your daughter and I'm asking you for her hand in marriage—so we can build our future together."

Stranton put his cup down. He wasn't surprised. In fact, he had expected the question to come soon; just not quite this soon. He hoped Raymond would have another year of law experience and more cases under his belt before they took such a major step in their lives. Stranton knew Cindy loved Raymond and it would be difficult to refuse giving his constant to the young lovers. While Stranton took his time—deep in thought—with a decision, Raymond's anxiety increased. Finally, Mr. Stranton broke the silence, saying, "Of course, I give my permission Raymond. What time frame are you looking at?"

"It all depends on Cindy and if she accepts my proposal."

Stranton grinned and wanted to say *Of course, she will, you fool!* His thoughts were interrupted as he heard Raymond add, "I'm taking her to the Persian House tonight for dinner and will present her with a ring. The money from my first case paid for the diamond. If she accepts, maybe it's a sign of good luck for future successes."

They both laughed as Raymond reached for the bill.

After lunch, Raymond returned to his office to complete a deposition and to meet a new client, Mr. Drew, who wanted to file a lawsuit against a big meatpacking company for misrepresentation. This could become another high-profile case. He glanced at his watch. It was 6:00 p.m. *I have just enough time to get home, shower, and make a quick change. I shouldn't meet with a new client so late in the day. Well, I can't afford to turn down new business, not with a potential wife entering my life.* He grabbed his hat and coat and hurried out the door. The chilly night announced an early fall.

His brownstone, in Gramercy Park, was a fifteen-minute walk from his office. He made the move from the village after joining the law firm. Moving up was part of his plan. As he reached the building, his neighbor, Mrs. Hurley was leaving. He tipped his hat. She smiled at the greeting and replied, "Good evening, Mr. Miller."

He opened the door and hurriedly took double steps up the long stairway to reach his apartment. The elevator was too slow and he needed to hurry. Raymond put on his new Hart and Schaffner navy pinstripe suit, white shirt, and red print necktie. *I need to make an especially good impression tonight.* Raymond always looked impeccable, and he knew that this impressed Cindy, as her father was the same way.

I hope Cindy's ready, Raymond thought, as he caught a cab to her home on the Upper East Side. It was a classier area for a Stranton and closer to her father's law firm. Someday, I'll be in the same league. As he rang the bell, he glanced at his watch. *I don't want to be late for our reservations at 8:00.* When the door quickly opened, he realized that, apparently, Cindy was also anxious about this evening. After all, not everyone dines at the Persian House. Raymond smiled as he saw her in the doorway. She looked radiant, draped in an elegant ankle-length pale-blue floral print silk dress with a low cut bodice. Her cleavage revealed enough breast to make Raymond feel moist. He longed to make love with Cindy instead of having dinner out; but this was their special night. He knew he had to contain his emotions for the time being. Maybe if he were lucky, they could complete the night at Cindy's apartment.

"You look irresistible, my darling," Raymond smiled at her.

"That's my intent," Cindy replied as she stepped on her tip-toes to kiss him. "I'll be just a moment."

The two lovebirds never noticed the strong November wind, as they walked to the restaurant arm in arm. Suddenly, Raymond stopped. "Cindy, look up at the sky all lined with flashing stars. Make a wish and send it to the Milky Way."

Cindy closed her eyes, waited a moment, took her hand to her lips and blew her wish towards the constellation.

"What was your wish?"

"If I tell you, it won't come true."

Just as Raymond was to inquire further, they reached their destination. The doorman opened the heavy wooden doors. Cindy walked into the room and gasped. "What opulence!"

"This place is swanky, Raymond, and pricey. It's going to set you back some. What's the occasion?"

"Oh, I don't know. I thought you deserved a special evening out for all your hard work on the Wilkens case."

Cindy smiled, "My father should think that way."

"He appreciates you, Cindy. He just doesn't relate it to you."

The maitre'd led them to a private corner booth. Cindy slid onto the red tufted velvet seat. She was dazzled by the glitter of hanging crystal chandeliers, beveled glass mirrors, and copies of statues from Roman artifacts. The big band sound of Glenn Miller was scheduled for 9:00. Raymond knew he had an hour to propose before the music drowned out his words of endearment as he popped the question. They ordered lobster dinners. While waiting, Raymond took Cindy's hands, looked intently into her eyes of azure, and inhaled the lemon scent of her golden hair that gracefully cascaded around her shoulders.

He said, "Cindy, we met in unusual circumstances. We endured three years of hard work together at NYU. As young students finding our way, I feel we've grown into mature adults with individual goals, but together we make a great couple. I believe our potential is unlimited. With life's challenges ahead of us, it is meaningless unless we're together, and you are by my side. Will you marry me?"

Then he reached into his jacket pocket and took out a small box. Cindy couldn't believe her eyes when she opened it. She had waited for this day since the moment he had introduced himself in the college library during their freshman year five years ago.

She took out a ring with a large round diamond surrounded by two baguettes. Raymond tenderly placed the ring on her finger. The diamonds glistened under the crystal lights, like evening stars. She thought, *The wish I sent to the galaxy tonight came true.*

"Oh, Raymond, it is so beautiful. Yes, darling, yes!"

She kissed him hard on the mouth. The waiter approached with Caesar salads and his presence became known when he gave a nervous cough. They both laughed as they parted to make room for the food.

"After our meal, I must call my parents and tell them the wonderful news," Cindy said. Raymond smiled, as he knew the

Strantons must already know. He summoned the waiter to bring a phone. Cindy dialed the number, praying silently that they were home. She repeated to herself: *Please be home, please be home* as the phone continued to ring. On the fourth ring, she heard her mother's voice. "Hello."

"Mom," she blurted out. "I'm engaged. I just received the most beautiful diamond ring from Raymond."

She held it up to admire its sparkle.

"That's wonderful news, Cindy. Will the two of you come to dinner tomorrow to celebrate and to show us the ring? I'll invite your brother and a few close friends. We can discuss an engagement party."

"Nothing too big, mother. Let me ask Raymond."

He nodded his head "yes," understanding the gist of the conversation. Cindy hung up and excused herself to go to the powder room. As she powdered her nose, her big smile reflected off the mirror telling her how lucky she was. She felt as if she were on cloud nine! Her thoughts ranged from her fast track career to, hopefully, winning the Wilkins case, and being engaged to the most wonderful man. She gave one last glance in the mirror before returning to their table. The band started to play Bing Crosby's song, *I've Got a Pocket Full of Dreams.*

"May I have this dance, darling Cindy?"

"Of course, my love. Let's make this our song."

As they twirled around the room, Cindy confessed that her mother wanted to have a formal engagement party for them. Raymond felt uncomfortable with the idea. All those people asking all kinds of questions. Going through with the wedding was enough. Yet he just didn't know how to refuse the Strantons' request. This night was too perfect to upset Cindy, so he agreed. As they danced intertwined in each other's arms, Raymond wished the evening would last forever. He wanted nothing to intrude on their happiness.

At midnight, they decided to leave and walk back to Cindy's apartment. She wrapped her fur around her shoulders, as the wind ripped her body.

"I feel rain or snow in the air. We'll have to get an earlier start to my home at the Grand Concourse tomorrow before a storm erupts."

"No problem," responded Raymond quietly. He escorted Cindy into the building. "Come in for a while. It's only half-past twelve."

Raymond hesitated. He was scared of his emotions. Cindy looked beautiful and sexy standing in the doorway. *How can I keep my hands off her?* He pondered.

"I better go home."

He bent down to kiss her goodnight, when she wrapped her arms around his waist and pulled him inside her apartment. As they kissed, she whispered, "Stay. Please stay." She started to take off his jacket and then his tie. The pace was rapid, their breathing hard. Their urgency increased. Raymond kept saying, "We need to stop."

Cindy kept repeating "Don't stop." Her blue dress easily slipped down to the floor. Raymond unhooked her brassiere and lifted each breast, gently sucking each nipple, until they were hard. He felt his organ swell. They fell onto the couch. He started kissing her neck, gradually traveling down to the pelvis, while, at the same time, he pulled off her panties. His mouth reached her vagina. His tongue darted in and out and swirled around the lips of the opening. Cindy groaned with pleasure. She had never felt such sensations. Her responses gave Raymond reassurance that he was igniting the right feelings. He tasted the salty moisture and inserted his finger to test her wetness. She was prime for insertion. Again he hesitated. This was so risky. "I want you. Don't hold back. Put your penis in," she cried out. Raymond's emotions overwhelmed him. He couldn't hold back. After all, he thought, we are getting married. He tried to be gentle as he entered her slowly yet masterfully. She was tight. She felt him inside. They moved in unison. The pain was brief; than they both felt an incredible euphoria. She was wet. She knew he came. Cindy was elated that she had pleased him. Exhausted, they fell asleep in each other's arms. In the morning when he found the red spot on the sheet, he knew he deflowered his love before their wedding night and felt a moment of sadness.

"I hope your parents never find out."

"That gives us all the reason to hasten the wedding plans."

Cindy showed no sign of regret. In fact, she added, "My feeling of completeness makes tonight's bliss worth any consequence that may occur."

Raymond grabbed her in his arms and kissed her hard on the lips and pushed his tongue into her mouth.

"I want your body again," he whispered. She withdrew. "There is plenty of time for more. But it's getting late. We need to get on the road."

Raymond wanted to stay in bed all day with his love and not listen to plans about dresses, décor, and wedding details. Usually, when Cindy's mind was set, there was no compromise.

"Let's stop by my apartment for a minute. I need to pick up some legal briefs for a new case. I can work in your dad's study until everyone arrives for dinner."

Cindy waited in the car. Raymond quickly climbed the stairs, opened the door, and easily located his papers. He carefully stuffed them into his briefcase and was back in the car within eight minutes.

"Boy, you are fast."

"Why not? I have a fair maiden waiting for me."

They chuckled and kissed, while Raymond quickly started the engine. They were on the road by 1:00 p.m.

Cindy relaxed in the seat while Raymond drove. She liked watching him behind the wheel. He was so sure of himself, so manly looking.

"So few people travel outside the city since the gas rationing," she stated as she looked around the nearly empty road. "Remember when dad handed me the keys to this sedan after I received my law degree? What fun escaping to the Catskills. We were so carefree. Now, since the war, I hoard the coupons and save them so we have enough for necessities. I wish the war would end."

What worried Cindy more was the possibility that Raymond might be drafted. Marriage would decrease his eligibility status and a child would certainly lower him on the induction scale. Raymond never voiced an opinion about being called for active duty, but he commented to her after the Japanese attacked Pearl Harbor and America declared war that being called into service was bad timing for his career. Cindy decided to bring up the subject to him.

"Raymond, I think it wise to marry as soon as possible, because of the escalation of troops into Europe."

He answered in surprise. "What do you mean?"

Cindy explained her concern about him being drafted if the war continued.

"I haven't given it a thought," he lied. That's all he thought about. If Uncle Sam called now, he might lose his big chance to build a practice and become famous like Mr. Stranton. He didn't want Cindy to think he was hungry for money and power or a coward to fight in the war, so he retorted:

"If our country calls, it's my duty to go."

Cindy was shocked by his reply, but proud of his patriotism.

He inquired, "How soon do you want to marry?"

"I was looking at April, if possible. That will give us six months to plan."

"Perfect. I don't like long engagements."

In regard to marriage status and being drafted, his mind actually worked like Cindy's. *What a relief,* she thought. *I was so worried he'd object and want to wait. Will mother think it's too soon for a proper, expensive, elegant wedding? I'll have a lot of persuading to do in this department.*

Cindy placed her head back and closed her eyes to relax and listen to her favorite tunes on the radio. When she finally opened them to check the time, she noticed the sky had turned dark gray. No more fluffy clouds and warm sun beating through the window. There was an eerie stillness, so different from the strong winds of last night. It seemed like the calm before the storm. Cindy started to feel uneasy and anxious. A torrential rain came spattering down as they pulled into the driveway. They ran quickly up the stairs to the front door.

"Mother! Dad! Is anyone home?" She shouted, looking around the house. Mrs. Stranton entered the living room.

"I'm here, I'm here. I was upstairs closing the windows. The downpour came so fast." She hugged her daughter.

"Hello, Raymond." She embraced him.

"Look, mother," Cindy beamed. She couldn't hold back her enthusiasm any longer.

Mrs. Stranton was surprised that Raymond had bought such a large diamond. *He must be doing better than I thought,* Mrs. Stranton surmised.

"It's beautiful, darling. Congratulations to both of you."

Cindy followed her mother into the kitchen talking a mile a minute about her ideas for the wedding. Raymond quietly disappeared into the library to work on the Shapiro case. At 4:00 o'clock, family and friends started to arrive. Raymond knew he had to stop his work. He piled all his papers back into his briefcase just as the door opened.

"So there you are, Raymond. Come join all the festivities in the parlor. We're making a toast to congratulate you and Cindy on your engagement."

Randall Stranton patted him on the back as they left the room to join everyone else. He had mixed drinks in a shaker and was passing them around. Raymond was handed a glass and guessed at its content. Randall raised his glass.

"To the young couple. May they have a lifetime of happiness."

Raymond was about to set his cocktail down, when Stranton came up to him, already a little tipsy from a few drinks.

"Come on, my boy; drink up. This toast is for you."

"I don't drink, sir."

"Be a man, Raymond. This is for your engagement."

Everyone was watching. Raymond put the glass to his lips. Dr. Debrinski's words came into his head: "DON'T take that first drink." It was such an awkward moment. He felt Cindy would misread his refusal to drink. He didn't want her to be disappointed in him and think he wasn't man enough to handle a few drinks. *If only I had told her the truth about my past,* he thought.

Cindy said "excuse me" to their neighbor, Mrs. Deutch, and started toward Raymond. Cindy had never seen him take a drink, but it was too late. The martini was down. It was smooth. Raymond felt the sensation as it trickled down his throat. *How I missed that taste!* At dinner, the wine glasses were filled and the toasts continued. Raymond was feeling good. His tension was gone. Just like the old days, the alcohol fortified his awkward social skills. The celebration was especially heartwarming for Raymond. He felt accepted by the Strantons. This was the beginning of his dream to be part of a loving family.

By the time the evening ended, the rain stopped. Raymond and Cindy needed to start back to the city.

"Maybe we should sleep over, Raymond, and start back early Monday."

"I can't, Cindy; I have an early appointment with my new client."

As they left, the cold air smacked them in the face.

"Put the heater on; I'm freezing," complained Cindy.

She started to feel uneasy, as Raymond took the curves rather quickly around the bend, before getting on the main road.

"Slow down, Raymond. You're going too fast."

Raymond wasn't hearing Cindy. His mind wasn't functioning properly. It felt foggy, his body numb. Was it the ice on the road, or his brain filled with alcohol? Raymond felt the car slide, and make a complete turnaround. He lost control, and slammed into a tree. His head hit the steering wheel, as the passenger door flew open and Cindy hit the ground on impact. Cindy's body didn't move. The car was smashed, the road dark and empty with two bodies lying alone, helpless. Raymond was unconscious and started to come to with a splitting headache. He felt dazed, confused. *What happened?* He held his head. He hobbled out of the car and saw Cindy on the ground.

"My God," he said, as he leaned down to see if she was still breathing. He felt a faint pulse. He started to cry. *What have I done?*

"Cindy, Cindy. Can you hear me? You can't die. I need you. I love you."

She didn't respond. *I've got to get help.* He took his coat off and covered her and started for the road. His ankle ached, but he ignored the pain. He approached the street and saw lights coming towards him. The car slowed down. It was Cindy's brother driving towards them.

"Raymond, what happened?"

"I don't know. I was driving and all of a sudden lost control of the car."

"Where's Cindy?"

"She's hurt, Daryl, really hurt."

Daryl ran towards the car and saw his sister lying there very still. "I'm going for help, Raymond. You stay here and don't leave."

Raymond sat on the ground next to his beloved, crying and praying frantically.

"I'm so sorry, Cindy. I didn't mean to hurt you. I shouldn't have taken that first drink."

Finally, in the background he heard the sirens. Help was on the way, but was it too late?

CHAPTER 27

▼

LIFE OR DEATH

Daryl Stranton waved the attendants down as the ambulance approached the embankment. He kept his car lights shining bright to lead them to the accident. Running to them, Daryl yelled, "Quick, my sister is lying unconscious by the tree."

They moved quickly, carrying a stretcher.

"Check her pulse, John."

"It's faint, but she's alive. Let's use a stabilizer and ease her up carefully," directed his husky, round-bellied partner. "She may have broken bones."

As they lifted Cindy into the ambulance, John noticed Raymond trembling. "Son, the cut over your eye looks bad. Let me take a look."

"No, I'm all right. Get Cindy to the hospital."

"Let me put this bandage on to stop the bleeding."

John quickly wrapped gauze around Raymond's head and jumped in the driver's seat of the ambulance.

"We'll follow you to Memorial's emergency room," Daryl told the driver. The police took Raymond aside for questioning.

"I don't know what happened, officer. I was driving towards Manhattan. The road was slick from all the rain and declining temperature. Before I realized the hazard, my car spun out of control and hit the tree."

"Were you drinking tonight?" the officer asked.

Raymond hesitated to answer. The officer looked up from his pad, waiting. Daryl was puzzled over Raymond's faltering. Daryl knew he had some drinks, but it didn't seem excessive. *Maybe he's in shock,* he reasoned. *However, I don't want to be detained any longer by a zealot officer.* Daryl quickly intervened.

"We made a toast to my sister and Raymond for their engagement earlier in the evening, but that was about all."

Raymond looked away and didn't say more.

"All right, you two can go to the hospital; and Mr. Miller, get that cut looked at. I'll contact you if more questions need answering. Right now, I'll call it an accident."

They thanked the officer and went to get into Daryl's car. Raymond's chest hurt and his right eye was throbbing. He could only concentrate on getting to Cindy. As they drove, Daryl pulled into a gas station.

"I'm calling my parents to tell them what happened."

The Strantons were asleep. When the phone rang, Randall reached for the receiver. "Hello," he said.

"Dad, this is Daryl. Cindy and Raymond were in an accident on their way home."

Mr. Stranton sat erect. "How bad is it?"

"Pretty bad for Cindy. She's unconscious."

"Good lord. Where'd they take her, Daryl?"

"To Memorial Hospital. Meet us there."

"We're on our way."

Daryl got back into the car driving slowly, due to the patches of ice. Raymond broke the silence.

"Daryl, I'm so sorry," he sobbed. "If Cindy dies, I don't want to live either."

"Calm down, Raymond. I think Cindy will come out of it. She's young, healthy, strong as a bull and stubborn as one."

Finally, a smile came to Raymond and he wiped his runny nose. The Strantons arrived as they approached the emergency room. Lucille ran to the nurse's station.

"I want to see my daughter, Cindy Stranton. The ambulance just brought her in."

"Calm down, Mrs. Stranton; the doctors are examining her and cleaning the wounds. They'll call you in when they're done."

"I want to see her now," she demanded.

"Okay, okay. Come with me, but no one else. The rest must stay in the waiting room."

The nurse took a look at Raymond and said, "Young man, you come with me." Raymond was led into another cubicle to wait for the attending doctor to look at his wound.

When Lucille looked at her daughter lying so still in bed, her heart broke.

"Cindy, Cindy, can you hear me? It's your mother." There was no response.

The physician, Dr. Fenton, tried consoling her.

"Mrs. Stranton, your daughter was knocked unconscious when she fell out of the car. We have to wait until her brain heals."

"Will she come out of it?"

"Only time will tell. Right now, we're taking her for X-rays to check for broken bones, and to make sure her neck and back are intact. Then she'll be assigned to a room."

They all watched the orderly roll the gurney down the hall and disappear around the corner. The Strantons waited in the lounge. Father and son paced, while Lucille tried to concentrate on reading a magazine. Raymond was X-rayed for broken ribs and stitched above his eye. He met up with the Strantons in Cindy's new room.

They all stayed until morning. Raymond dozed on a chair. Mr. Stranton and Daryl slumped in the corners of the couch, while Lucille spent most of the night weeping. She thought, *How beautiful and gifted my daughter is and now she lies in bed fighting for her life.* At the break of dawn, the noise of hospital chores and chatter woke the weary visitors. They looked at Cindy, but no change had occurred.

"There's no point in us waiting, Raymond. I'll drive you home," suggested Daryl. "The doctors don't know when she'll awake. It could be days."

"No, I don't want to leave."

Mr. Stranton put his arm around Raymond's shoulder. "Son, my wife will stay. I'm going to the office with Daryl. You need to go home and get cleaned up. If there are any changes, Lucille will call me and I will call you."

Finally, Raymond agreed. Just as the three turned to leave the room, a voice called out and Cindy's eyes opened.

"Mom, Dad, what am I doing here? I can't move my legs. They're numb. Why am I in such pain?"

"Quick: find the doctor, Daryl."

Raymond's eyes swelled. He froze on the spot. *How can I look Cindy in the face? It's all my fault. I caused her pain.* She saw Raymond standing there.

"Darling, come here. Tell me what happened."

As he approached, she became alarmed.

"You're hurt. Look at your face."

"It's nothing; just a few stitches and a few cracked ribs."

He choked up thinking, *Just like Cindy worrying about me, while she's in bed unable to move. What do I say to her? What do I do? Dad isn't here to help me out of this mess.* Raymond sat on the side of the bed and caressed her hand. He bent down and started to kiss her forehead and then lips.

"Forgive me, Cindy; please forgive me."

"Tell me what happened."

He proceeded with the same story he had told the police, Daryl, and the Strantons, but he left out one vital part: *the affects of alcohol on an alcoholic. Yes, that's what I am*, he admitted to himself. *Even after five years of sobriety. I took the first fatal drink that Dr. Debrinski warned me about and then let them repeatedly refill my wine glass. Why was I so weak to let them manipulate me into drinking again? I betrayed my sweetheart.*

"Raymond," he heard Cindy in the distance, as his mind was clouded in thought. "It was an accident. How can I blame you?"

Raymond buried his head on her shoulder thinking, *I don't deserve this wonderful woman.*

The doctors came running to examine Cindy. They didn't like the scenario. They took a pin and pricked her legs and feet. There was no sensation. They looked sternly at each other.

"Let's get her back to X-ray," ordered Dr. Fenton. "We need pictures of her lower back."

They rolled her onto a gurney and started down the hall. Cindy called out to Raymond and her family.

"All of you go and get your work done. This will take awhile. I'll be all right. Come back later. Maybe they'll have some results."

Her mother stayed in the waiting room wearing a face of concern, expecting the worst. The others left as Cindy requested, promising to return that evening. Cindy wasn't allowed to move on the table, as they took picture after picture of her spinal column concerned what the outcome could mean for this young woman.

Mrs. Stranton ran to her daughter and grabbed her hand as they wheeled her back to the room. Dr. Fenton followed.

"What did the X-rays show, doctor?"

"I want to consult with a neurologist before we come to any conclusions. He needs to look at the results and examine your daughter. I contacted Dr. Reimer. Hopefully, he'll come to the hospital this afternoon. The X-rays should be dry. We'll meet in Cindy's room by early evening if everything goes accordingly."

"Will she walk again, Dr. Fenton?"

"Let's wait and talk later. Right now, we're placing her on a rigid backboard and she needs to be turned every two hours. We don't want any bed sores to develop."

Dr. Fenton left and the two women were alone.

"This isn't really happening to me, mother. It's all a dream. When I wake up, I'll be fine," Cindy whispered.

She didn't really believe those words, but she couldn't face reality.

"Mother, why me? Why did it happen to me? If I can't walk, how can I go on? Clients don't want an invalid as their attorney. What kind of a wife can I make Raymond? I can't even pee by myself."

As Cindy cried, all these questions rushed out at Lucille, leaving her in a guarded situation. *I want to say something optimistic to Cindy. How can I? I feel dread and despair.*

Finally, Cindy calmed down and fell asleep. *I wonder if it's all the pain medication or if her hysterics wore her out,* thought Mrs. Stranton. She slipped out of the room to get some coffee and called her husband to relay Dr. Fenton's conversation.

"We'll return to the hospital by 6:00 p.m.," stated Mr. Stranton. "Don't be late, darling. I want you to hear the outcome of Cindy's condition."

Next, Mrs. Stranton called the Acme Nursing Agency to hire a private nurse for Cindy. She needed too much attention to be left alone and Lucille wanted to return home to catch up on some sleep. The hospitals were short-staffed due to the war. So many nurses had gone to the front.

Promptly that evening, the men returned to Memorial and gathered in Cindy's room waiting to meet with the doctors. Everyone was scared to hear the report, but they needed to know the results. It was 7:00 o'clock when Dr. Fenton and Dr. Reimer appeared. Introductions were exchanged and Dr. Reimer, a tall slender man with hair slightly graying at the temples, proceeded to explain Cindy's condition.

"When Cindy was thrown from the car, she badly bruised her spinal cord in the lower sacral area. This affected her hips and legs and that's why she's paralyzed. Her upper body remained intact, which is good. Presently, cardiac and respiratory problems aren't an issue. However, her bodily functions are hampered and she's using a urinary catheter to empty her bladder. We must be vigilant and monitor for urinary tract infections. Within a few days when the swelling goes down, we'll know if Cindy obtains any movement back to her lower extremities."

"And if I don't, Dr. Reimer?"

"Then you will need to depend on a wheelchair for mobility."

"Is that what you call a paraplegic, Dr. Reimer?"

"Cindy, you can learn to have a functional life. A great majority of paraplegics do adjust. They return to work and have fulfilling family and social lives."

"Ah, you mean people take pity on them."

"That's not what I mean, Cindy and you know it."

"What about the pain, doctor? I've never experienced pain like this. I can only describe it as a deep, burning, tingling sensation that engulfs the paralyzed area."

"We'll give you pain medication to control it."

Cindy felt anger surfacing and knew she was taking her frustrations out on the doctor. *I sound nasty. Shame on me*, she thought. *I like him. He shows kindness while his voice expresses authority.*

Mr. Stranton spoke up. "We want the best for her, Dr. Reimer, bar no expenses."

"I understand, Mr. Stranton, but right now she needs rest to give her spine time to heal. Your daughter will be in the hospital for a long time. If she regains mobility in her legs, we might recommend rehabilitation at New York State Reconstruction Home. It is thirty-five minutes north of the city in the heart of the Hudson Valley. With braces, your daughter might return to walking. For now, she's confined to bed."

The doctors proceeded to leave. Cindy started to cry out.

"I'm no good anymore. I just want to die."

Raymond left the room. He couldn't stand to see his beloved so upset and discouraged. Cindy's father approached the bed and put his arms around his daughter. "You'll get better, Cindy. I promise."

"What if I don't? Society won't see me being productive. They'll see me as a cripple."

"Then show them you have no limitations. Show your tenacity and what you can accomplish."

Cindy had heard enough. She closed her eyes to escape into darkness and quickly fell asleep. Her private nurse arrived and the entourage left.

CHAPTER 28

▼

TRAUMATIC DECISION

As Detective Pierce sat in his office drinking black coffee with two lumps of sugar, he noticed an article in the *Detroit Times* that caught his attention. He called over McQuire.

"Look here. It looks like our boy finally slipped up again." McQuire read the headline: "Prominent New York attorneys involved in auto accident."

"So what does that have to do with us?"

"Read the article, McQuire. What is the name of one of the lawyers?"

"Holy shit! Raymond Miller, Jr."

"Is that Senator Miller's son?"

"One and the same. I think I should fly to New York and question this Cindy Stranton about the accident."

"The boss isn't going to let you go. Besides, how are you going to link this accident with the old case in Detroit?"

"Maybe Raymond told Miss Stranton about the other accident or maybe she's so mad about what happened to her that she will divulge information without intending to."

"I doubt that. I hear she's a hotshot attorney about to marry Mr. Miller. I don't think she will even talk to you."

"Let's see about that. I'll take the first flight out tomorrow morning and be back by evening. I think the boss will give me one day off. You can cover for me now that you've been promoted from officer to detective."

McQuire just shook his head. "Just forget it. Too much time has elapsed."

But Pierce was persistent, especially since he felt tricked by the Millers. His gut told him Raymond was guilty of the first accident and somehow caused this one. Proving it was going to be tough.

Pierce boarded the 7:00 a.m. plane for La Guardia and arrived at the hospital before visiting hours. He showed the head nurse his badge and was escorted into Cindy's room. Cindy was in bed waiting for the nurse to rotate her again. Pierce introduced himself and tried to explain why he was there.

"I don't understand," Cindy said. "You mean Raymond was involved in another accident in Detroit when he was young? But if he was the cause, why didn't you arrest him?"

"We didn't have proof. He left the scene of the accident and then disappeared, car and all. His influential father covered up for him. We were led to believe he was somewhere in Europe attending college."

"Raymond attended NYU Law School."

"So he was right here in New York all this time. Miss Stranton, this is an important question. Please think hard. Is Raymond a drinker?"

"No, absolutely not. In fact, I've known him for five years and never seen him take a drink. Why do you ask?"

She didn't reveal his drinking the night of the dinner.

"When he was younger, he was a heavy drinker. I'd classify him as an alcoholic. I think alcohol caused the first accident and his father sent him somewhere to dry out. There was no trace of him until I read in the newspaper that he was the attorney who won the Bravo case. I haven't visited his first victim for a long time, but he left her for dead. The last time I inquired, she was walking with a brace. Now I see you lying here and too many frightening memories come back. What Raymond didn't understand and maybe still doesn't is that having a car accident is tragic enough, but driving drunk and having an accident is malice."

Cindy held back the tears, but was ready to explode.

"I'm sorry, Detective Pierce; I can't help you. I think you have the wrong man, because my Raymond isn't capable of doing what you say this person did."

"You don't know that, Miss Stranton. He was a very young unhappy individual at that time."

"Please leave. I don't want to discuss this anymore."

"Here's my card. If you change your mind or are willing to talk, I would appreciate a call."

Pierce left and Cindy could no longer hold back the gush of tears from her eyes. *Now it all fits in. Why Raymond was so mys-*

terious about his past. He hid everything from me. How can I ever trust him again?

Cindy felt betrayed: stripped from showing emotions towards another human being. *How could the love of my life be the cause of this disaster? If I had known his past, I would have insisted that we stay the night at mom and dad's. We did a lot of toasting. I even felt lightheaded, but he said he was fine. Some happy couple we are now.* Lucille walked in as Cindy rehashed in her mind what went wrong at their engagement celebration.

"Hi, darling. What's wrong? You look unsettled. Is something troubling you?"

"Oh, nothing mother; just the unexpected perils of life."

"You have that funny look on your face."

"What look is that?"

"It's your tough 'get even' look."

Cindy ignored her mother's comments.

"When Raymond comes this evening, would you make sure we're alone for a while? I want to talk with him privately."

"Now, Cindy, don't say anything rash. Think everything over."

"I did, mother, the whole morning. I thought my situation over very carefully."

Cindy didn't tell her mother about the visitor. She wanted to handle Raymond herself without family interference. However, the longer she waited for him to visit, the more she seethed over his deception.

Raymond left the office early to get to Cindy by 5:00 p.m. before other family members visited. He missed her and wanted to let her know how much. When he arrived in the room, he bent down to kiss her mouth, but she turned her face. He thought it strange and became concerned that she might be in pain.

"Darling, how did your day go?"

"The morning was very interesting. I had a visitor from Detroit. You know; your hometown."

Startled, Raymond sat down without commenting, but his pallor revealed his inner turmoil.

"Don't you want to know the name?"

"I figured you'll tell me."

"Are you familiar with the name Pierce?"

"Not really."

"*Detective* Pierce."

Raymond swallowed hard and tried not to show any emotion. He felt his heart palpitate.

"What did this Pierce come to see you about?"

"Oh, come off it, Raymond. You remember your shenanigans about seven years ago. Pierce explained your big-time drinking, erratic driving, traffic tickets, minor accidents, and then the hit-and-run disaster."

"Cindy, I—"

"Don't say a word. If you had told me about your past, I would have understood and tried to help."

"No, you wouldn't. You would have condemned me like all the others."

"Well, now, I despise you!" She took off her ring and threw it at him. "You've maimed two women and you will have to live with that."

"Cindy, I love you. It was an accident. I lost control because of the ice, not alcohol. I would never jeopardize your safety."

"I told you to slow down. You were going too fast, but you didn't listen. I look at my limp body and I feel hate. Now get out."

There was nothing more to be said. Raymond felt devastated. He got up, put his coat on, and left. This time Cindy didn't shed any tears. Instead, she vowed to endure treatment and come back a stronger person. *I will return to work and make a new life for myself whether I walk or not.*

Lucille Stranton watched from the lounge as Raymond ran out of Cindy's room. She felt something was horribly wrong. As she returned to her daughter to inquire what happened, Lucille noticed that Cindy's engagement ring was missing. She knew this wasn't an appropriate time to pump her for information. *Cindy will tell me in good time*, she reassured herself.

CHAPTER 29

▼

NO ALTERNATIVES

Raymond ran out of the hospital feeling destroyed. His head pounded, his stomach churned, and his body felt drained. He thought, *What happened that my life is so messed up?* He entered the subway and waited for the "D" train to travel back to Manhattan. He got off at Battery Park and climbed the steps to street level. At the corner was Hal's Bar. He passed by so many times, but never walked in. There was no need then. Today was different. He needed a drink to deal with the loss of Cindy. He felt so alone. Raymond entered and grabbed a stool at the bar.

"Give me a bourbon on the rocks."

He didn't stop at one. He kept drinking, thinking enough booze would erase the pain. Just before midnight, Raymond stumbled out of Hal's. He fell near a cardboard statue and leaned on it to lift himself up. Through his blurred vision, he saw a man's silhouette draped in stripes, wearing a top hat covered with stars. A finger pointed at him. Raymond read, "I want you." *Someone still wants me, he concluded.* Feeling nauseous and retching his guts out on the street, Raymond thought, *I've got to get home.* He started walking, bumping into poles, and decided to hail a taxi. "Driver, take me to Gramercy Park." Miraculously, he recognized his building, paid the driver, and got out. He fumbled up the stairs, tripping several times until he reached his apartment, and then opened the door. Once inside, he passed out on the bed and never woke up until morning.

As the sun baked through the grimy windows, Raymond tried to open his eyes and focus. *My head is killing me.* The pressure banged against his temples. *I need coffee*, he thought, and reached for the pot. After five cups, he showered and dressed. The clock showed 10:00 a.m. *I need to reach my office, but first I have a stop to make.* Raymond went back to the sign he saw at Hal's Bar. Uncle Sam was calling and he was willing to oblige. *If I don't do something with my life, I'm going to end up an alcoholic living in the Bowery.* Raymond opened the door to the recruiting office and enlisted in the army. Next, he went to his office and started packing. He made an appointment to meet with Mr. Tate to discuss his resignation.

"I don't understand, Raymond. Are you not happy here?"

"I was very happy, sir, but unexpected circumstances have changed that."

"I heard about Cindy and I'm so sorry, but she'll get better. Give it time."

"It's more complicated than that, sir."

"You were my budding attorney with such aspirations. Raymond, don't spoil your career. You can make it big."

"The army needs me and maybe I can get me some Japs and make a difference in the war."

"Well, if I can't change your mind, let me at least wish you good luck."

They shook hands and Raymond left. On the street, he took in a deep breath and for the first time enjoyed the crisp cold air of November, 1942. *Next, I need to tell my landlord I'm leaving.* He packed a few possessions in a duffle bag and threw out some stored junk. *Thank goodness the apartment came furnished and I don't have any worldly valuables.* The next step was the hardest: picking up the phone to call home. He hadn't spoken to his parents since the day he called to tell them he was engaged. It seemed so long ago. *Everyone was happy and making plans. Now, the plans only include me.* The phone rang and he heard his dad say, "Hello."

"Hello, dad; this is Raymond."

"Raymond, I've been trying to get you for days. We've been out-of-town and when we came back, I received a message that you and Cindy were in an accident. Are you both all right?"

"Well, it's like this, dad: I fucked up my life. Cindy's in the hospital paralyzed. She blamed me for the accident because I had a few drinks. But I wasn't drunk, dad. It was icy and my car slid into a tree. Then, Detective Pierce read about it in the *Detroit Times* and came to New York to fill Cindy in on all the gory details of my past. She blew up, because I didn't confide in her and kicked me out of her life. So, dad, I called to say goodbye to you and mom. I joined the army. I can't lie or hide anymore. I'm going to serve my country. Maybe I can make up for all my sins."

"What about your career? You were on your way to becoming a famous attorney."

"You never understood me, dad. That doesn't mean anything without Cindy. Maybe one day she'll learn to forgive me. After the war, I'll return and see if we can start over again. Goodbye, dad. Let me say goodbye to mom."

Before retiring to bed, Raymond went to call Cindy to say farewell and send good wishes, but she hung up the phone after hearing his voice. The next day he was shipped to Fort Bragg for training.

The nights were hard for Cindy, and unless doped with pain medication, she couldn't sleep. She felt so lonely since sending Raymond away. On the night Raymond left, she felt restless and edgy and the pills weren't helping. She waited for the nurse to come and rotate her in bed. Cindy wondered, *Where is Miss Snyder? She is late.* Out of frustration, Cindy tried to move her leg and thought she felt some motion. She was excited, yet hesitated to say anything and get her hopes up. When the nurse showed up, Cindy didn't utter a word. The next morning, she was able to wiggle her toes and raised her legs slightly off the bed. Cindy yelled for her nurse. Ruth Snyder came running.

"What is it, Cindy?"

"Please get the doctor. I think I gained back some movement in my legs."

Snyder ran to get Dr. Fenton. He came to examine Cindy. He pricked her feet with a pin and she yelled "ouch." *This is my happiest moment,* she thought.

"I think the swelling is going down and sensations are coming back. I'll contact Dr. Reimer to come and examine you. Don't get too attached to your wheelchair. I don't think you will need it."

Cindy was so ecstatic over this new revelation that her first thought was to call Raymond. She picked up the phone, and then returned the receiver to its cradle. *I'll wait until I can walk again and surprise him. I don't care about his past. I love Raymond too much to be without him.*

CHAPTER 30

▼

UNEXPECTED NEWS

On August 14, 1945, World War II ended. The country was in transition. Becky's private war with her emotions was resolved and an uneasy calm settled in the Abrom home. Becky's psychiatrist was paid in full and medical expenses decreased. For the next nine years, the Abroms returned to a routine. Becky volunteered at a Jewish agency to assist Holocaust survivors and European refugees immigrating to the United States. Finding housing, furniture, and clothing helped them assimilate into Detroit's Jewish community. Nate joined Al Green Enterprises at Willow Run Airport, where he baked for their restaurant during the fifties. Rena worked full-time in billing at the Mills Paint Company and Dena entered Durfee Junior High School. The family was able to accumulate some money. Stability returned as Becky maintained the household.

It was Friday afternoon and Becky was in the kitchen cooking Sabbath dinner when the pain intensified. The itching increased and she wanted to rip the skin off her leg. The redness intensified around the shiny thin skin covering her right leg. A brilliant blue vein rippled through the scar like a lighting rod. When Nate woke from his nap and went into the kitchen to help his wife, she turned almost in tears. "Look how inflamed my leg is."

Nate didn't like what he saw and said in a concerned tone, "You're on your feet too much. Let me rub your leg with alcohol after dinner; maybe it will reduce the radiating heat." The relief was short-lived.

"Becky, make an appointment with Dr. Lossman, and let him tell you what to do."

"I'm afraid. What if I have to go into the hospital? I won't go under the knife again. The cost! We just got out of debt and started to save. You need a car. How long can you travel by bus to the airport at midnight?"

"You worry too much. Maybe the doctor will give you a cream to take the redness away. Just make an appointment. We'll pay whatever the cost; we always have."

The following week, Becky went to see her internist. He was taken aback by the change in the appearance of Becky's leg.

"When did it start looking so inflamed?"

"About a month ago."

"I want you to see a specialist. Something is definitely wrong. I believe the best orthopedic doctor in Detroit is Dr. Peter

Richman. Call right away and make an appointment. I'll write a referral letter and give him some background on your case."

Two weeks later, Becky and Nate went to see Dr. Richman. His office was packed with young and old, and children wearing casts. After an hour's wait, the nurse called the Abroms into an inner office. It took another fifteen minutes before the doctor came in. The slight, medium height gentleman with a soft voice and gentle manner started to examine Becky's leg. She took to his kindness right away.

"How long has it been since the accident?"

"Nineteen years," replied Becky.

"Have you been active in those years?"

"I guess."

Nate added, "She's never off her feet, doctor."

"From what Dr. Lossman wrote and what I see, I would say your leg is wearing out. I hope I can be honest with you, Mrs. Abrom."

"Of course, doctor. No holding back."

"The skin protecting the inner plate is deteriorating. If something isn't done to cover the wound, it will tear open and gangrene will set in. Then it'll be too late. I'll have to amputate."

"No. I'm not losing my leg."

"Then surgery is your only answer. If you leave it alone, eventually the poison will take over your body and you will die. I don't mean to scare you, but you must know the truth."

Becky's face revealed fear. "What kind of surgery would you do?"

"The only way to save your leg is through grafting. I have to admit it's experimental, but if it works, you'll make history and add a new dimension to this type of surgery."

"Could you explain the operation?"

"First, you need two short hospital stays to prepare the leg for grafting. The major surgery takes eight to ten hours. I will take the skin from the back of your left leg and grow it on the other to cover the plate. Then, I'll graft skin from your stomach to fill in the hollow part of the left leg. The legs are held together by a square wooden frame and suspended in the air. A cast keeps the legs in place. A trapeze hangs from a metal rod, so you can pull your upper body up as needed. You will be bedridden for six to eight weeks."

Nate and Becky looked at each other stunned and speechless. They had never heard of such an ordeal. Becky thought: *I had to endure all this pain and suffering because of a careless drunk driver.* Coming back to reality, she said, "When do we get started, doctor?"

"Don't you want to go home and think about it?"

"I have no choice. I fought so hard to save my leg from age twenty-one that I'm not going to lose it at forty."

"I'll need X-rays and some tests. Why don't you start making appointments with Gail, our receptionist?"

Gail asked, "Mr. Abrom, do you have insurance?"

Nate proudly handed her his Blue Cross card.

"I'm worried it won't cover the costs because of the preexisting condition clause," he said.

"I understand, but gangrene is a new diagnosis, so the surgery will be covered," Gail said. Relieved, they left for home to prepare the girls on the newest development. At dinner, Rena and Dena listened and seemed perplexed, but they knew the drill. When Mom goes into the hospital, it's their responsibility to take over the household.

In October, 1954, the preliminaries were completed and surgery was scheduled. Enough time was allowed for healing before the seasonal holidays; that is, if everything went well. On the day of the operation, Nate and the girls waited in the lounge for practically the whole day.

"Daddy, what could be taking so long? I'm worried," Dena fretted.

"Don't worry: the doctor told me it's a long procedure."

Nate was getting concerned. Rena didn't say much. They went down to the cafeteria to eat lunch, later had a snack, and tried reading magazines. Finally, ten hours later, Dr. Richman came to inform them that the surgery went well.

"How she handles the recuperation will tell if the ending is successful."

They didn't quite understand what he meant until they saw Becky in the room. As the family entered, Dena whispered to her sister, "I can't believe it. Mother looks like a hanging body in a slaughter house."

Rena ignored her sister. She was too upset to speak. Nate ran to his wife trying to assist her in any way he could. She was still groggy from the anesthesia and her mouth seemed parched.

"Here, Becky; maybe some ice chips will keep your lips moist."

Nate traveled an hour daily by bus to New Grace Hospital in northwest Detroit to visit his wife. He came home, ate dinner, napped, got up, and traveled another hour to work with no complaints. Nate was totally devoted. For him, it was the natural and right thing to do.

On the third day post-surgery, Becky couldn't wait to tell Nate what happened to Dr. Richman's twenty-year-old patient, Danny, who had had grafting similar to hers.

"Nate, you won't believe it, but Danny couldn't take the pain any longer, so he tried to grab the hanger on the nightstand to rip off his cast and fell out of bed and broke his hip. I guess he's not seasoned to pain like me. After all that surgery, this episode set him back quite a bit."

Becky hung in there no matter what the pain or discomfort. Preserving her leg was the motivating factor. *It has to work*, she kept telling herself. When her door was opened, strangers passing in the hall poked their head in the room to say hello, and to see the contraption that held Becky's leg together for eight weeks.

After discharge from the hospital, the road to recuperation was long and tedious. From the surgeon's point-of-view, the outcome was successful and Dr. Richman explained to Becky that her case would be written up in an orthopedic medical journal. There were, however, some negative outcomes for the patient. First, the stomach grafting to fill in the back of her left leg didn't totally work. A big indentation was left. Secondly, her stomach felt raw and sensitive. Anything touching the area was painful, so panties were bought two sizes too big. Before the surgery, she had one good leg and one bad. Now both legs were affected, but it didn't matter. Becky still had two limbs to walk on, which kept her on the road of independence. The rest she would endure.

CHAPTER 31

▼

OPPORTUNITIES

By the mid fifties, the Abrom family took their chance to share the American dream by making two big purchases all for the sake of Becky's health. The focus after Becky's grafting was preserving her leg. It didn't surprise her when Nate broached the subject.

"Becky, you need to cut down on your walking and doing laundry in the basement. The dampness and steps are harming your leg. This house is no longer suited for us."

Becky was aware of how many people were moving out of the neighborhood, because of the change in housing designs, freeways, and malls.

"Nate, you know our neighbors Frances and Rose? They talked about buying their own home in Northwest Detroit. The houses they looked at were new and had backyards, but the prices are too high for our budget. I'm told further out at the baseline of Detroit and outlying towns, called suburbs, single family dwellings are in demand. Maybe there are some no-basement houses, because that's what I'll need. We also need money for a down payment, which we won't have if we buy a car this year."

"First, we buy the car, Becky, to cut down on your walking. Next year, we'll have more money saved and I'll ask my brother or father to give us a loan."

The girls were flabbergasted when they heard their parents were purchasing an automobile. Rena gasped, "I never thought I'd see the day mother would give in to buying a car."

"The spell is broken. The automobile is no longer the enemy," exclaimed Dena. "We can be like everyone else. Buy that pretty pale pink color!"

Becky and Nate just smiled at each other. They had the color all picked out.

A week later, Mr. and Mrs. Abrom walked into the dealership to pick up their beauty. After twenty years of not owning a car, they drove up to their flat in a shiny new 1955 turquoise-and-white Ford Fairlane four-door sedan, with large white-wall tires. This was a day of celebration. First, the girls came running out, then the Wilburs and other neighbors walked over to examine what they saw. So many wishes of good luck went around that Nate and Becky felt proud of their accomplishment.

Dena shouted, "Next year, I'm getting a driving permit. Daddy, Will you teach me how to drive?"

"Of course."

But Rena, like her mother, was too scared.

"I'm never driving," she told Dena. "I don't trust the other drivers on the road."

Another year went by and Becky felt her legs throbbing when she went down to wash clothes. She knew a decision to move was in the near future. She looked in the newspaper and asked people on the block where to go for new housing.

Her neighbor, Sadie, said, "Becky, look at houses in Northwest Detroit, around the Eight Mile and Lahser area, or Oak Park and Southfield. That's where my relatives are looking since they can't afford Palmer Woods or Sherwood Forest. That's where I'm going when I leave this block."

Sadie added, "There is a new shopping complex in the area called Northland Mall. I heard it's unbelievable. You can drive there and park free in a huge parking lot. Once you move out that way, you won't shop downtown any more. No more meeting friends under the Kern's clock."

Becky couldn't wait to tell Nate about all the housing opportunities waiting in the suburbs.

"Nate, Can we look this weekend?"

They decided to drive out Sunday, after Nate got up from his afternoon nap. On their excursion, they noticed how different the suburbs were from urban living. There were ranch-style houses standing in a row and small trees planted by the street. There were pockets of neighborhood shopping with a supermarket, drugstore, deli, and other independent stores. Becky noticed all the open land on Eight Mile Road.

"I feel so far out from the city."

Their last stop was a subdivision across from the Ivory Polo Grounds at Eight Mile and Lahser Road.

"I can't believe we're looking at houses with horse stables two blocks away," Nate marveled.

"Don't worry; they are selling the property and the polo grounds are moving within a year."

"You hope, Becky. This is country living."

"That's what we said about your sister Dorothy's house on Seven Mile and Greenfield Road. Now look how that area is built up. Besides, it's a perfect house for us and only $12,000. The utility room and kitchen are so big and the pull-down ladder in the utility room leads to extra attic storage. The girls can have their own bedroom. We can fix it up really cute. Look how big the yard is. You can grow vegetables or have a flower garden."

"Let's go home and I'll call my family to see if I can borrow some money. I'll go to the bank to learn the best way to finance the house."

Nate called his brother Lawrence and explained that he needed a loan for a down payment on a house. Lawrence said, "I'll think about it." A few days later, he called to say no. His father didn't think they needed to move and he said he didn't have it. Nate knew different. Becky was furious when she heard the outcome.

"I can't believe it. When I was sick and you worked two and three jobs and needed money, we never asked for a dime. Now, when we ask for a little help, they say no. Well, the hell with them. I'll never ask them for anything ever again."

Dena wasn't surprised to see her mother so upset. Her mother was always too proud to ask for help from an agency like Jewish Family Services, even when they were in dire need. Becky feared the neighbors would find out and she would feel ashamed.

The next day, Nate went to the bank to inquire about a mortgage.

"Are you a veteran, Mr. Abrom? They have the GI bill, where you can buy a house for no money down."

"No, that won't work."

"Maybe we can work something out with an FHA mortgage, although if your down payment is low, your monthly payment will be higher."

"See what figures you come up with and I'll be back."

Becky and Nate sat down that evening to figure their finances. It would be tight and they also needed money for appliances, carpeting, storm windows, and screens. Nate would put in his own grass. After figuring and refiguring, they decided it would work. *Maybe Rena can pay a little more for room and board. In three years, Dena will graduate high school and find a job. She could contribute to the budget.* Becky added more payment envelopes to keep her bookkeeping system viable. Somehow the family pooled together to make their dream come true.

CHAPTER 32

▼

SAYING GOODBYE

Moving day was difficult for the Abroms. Friends, relatives, and relationships drifted in and out through the years, but Monterey Street was the circle of security, the place where neighbors aided Becky during her bouts of illness. It was the only house her kids knew and their family lived close by. Bubbie Bertha maintained family bliss for five years prior to Papa Hooberman's fatal heart attack, at age seventy-two. There were family dinners, parties, dinners out, seeing movies, or just visiting at each others' homes. In that time, the Abroms attended half-brother Sammy's wedding and made acquaintances with half-sister Rona's first born. When relations ended again for the final time, it severed unions between half-sisters, half-brothers, aunts, uncles, and cousins. Becky made closure, but in her heart a loneliness lingered on.

Most of Nate's family had already moved to the suburbs, except for one sister and his dad. Benny lived in a small apartment above a store on Linwood and had no intentions of moving. He lived in squalor, but had money hidden in nooks and crannies, and was content. *The hardest thing about leaving,* thought Becky, *was leaving Aunt Mary and her sister. We said goodbye a dozen times.*

The move took place in June, 1956, just after Dena graduated from Durfee. This would give her enough time to adjust to the new neighborhood before starting Redford High School. The transition was hard because all her friends went to either Mumford or Oak Park High School. Being the new kid on the block and attending a new school was difficult because Dena was one of a handful of Jews at her new school. It wasn't like the old schools. At Redford, some kids had never met a Jewish person. That didn't stop Dena. To her, kids were kids, and she made friends easily. Dena experienced the best three years of her school life.

CHAPTER 33

▼

BIG MISTAKE

Two months had passed since the accident and Cindy started to see progress in her walking. The pain eased and her medication decreased. Fortunately, new surroundings at the New York Rehabilitation facility provided her with much motivation. It was no longer just sick people in a hospital. She no longer felt helpless, just lonely. How she pined for Raymond's touch and kisses. Cindy yearned for his kind words and support. *I was too harsh with him*, she thought. *I didn't give him a chance to explain. It was anger that took over, not rational thinking. I hope he can forgive me. When I get out of here, I'll walk into his office and surprise him.*

Why am I nauseous each morning? I don't remember feeling that way before. My breasts are tender and my waist feels wider. I gained a few pounds, but it must be from my immobility. As she lay in bed after therapy, Cindy thought about some wonderful moments with Raymond like the night they became engaged and later at her apartment, when they embraced and made love. *Oh my God, these symptoms I'm having; it can't be happening. I can't be pregnant.* She was too frightened to tell anyone, especially her mother. *How do I explain we were in love, engaged, and about to be married? When our bodies melted together, it felt like heaven. We never considered possible consequences. Think, Cindy, think. I need to discreetly find a gynecologist to give an examination and pregnancy test.*

When her physical therapist came the next day, she took her aside and asked: "Denise, I am having some itching and burning when I urinate. Is it possible to see a doctor for an exam?"

"Sure. You might need penicillin for an infection. I'll get Dr. Gibson to see you."

"I prefer a female doctor for my problems."

"We don't have one in the rehab hospital."

"Recommend someone to come. I'll get the money and pay privately."

The therapist looked puzzled. *Why is she so insistent on a gynecologist for a bladder infection?* Denise looked in the hospital directory for a doctor on staff that came occasionally to see pregnant patients. She put in a call to Dr. Stryker. He could see Miss Stranton next week. Cindy was beside herself with worry. *What if I'm having a baby and I sent the father away? Think clearly. I could go to a private clinic and abort the child. I could call Raymond and explain he's going to be a father; or leave town, have the baby, and give it up for adoption. I know I'll have the baby and raise it myself with help from my parents and nannies. Money isn't an issue. The child would remind me of the love Raymond and I once shared. What would mother say?*

When Dr. Stryker arrived, Cindy explained her dilemma to him in strict confidence. *I need time to make a decision if the test comes back positive.* He reassured her of his discretion. A week later the results came back as Cindy feared. She already figured out the path to take. Cindy picked up the phone to call Raymond, but the line was dead—disconnected. Frightened, she called his office. After the secretary said, "Hello," Cindy responded: "May I speak to Raymond Miller, Jr.?"

"I'm sorry. Mr. Miller is no longer with us."

"Where did he go?"

"We cannot divulge that information."

"This is Cindy Stranton, his fiancée." Cindy couldn't believe she still called herself that.

"I'm sorry, company policy; it's out of my hands."

Sandra Sloan thought, *Odd. Why doesn't she know where he is if she's engaged to him?* Sandra politely said goodbye and hung up. By now, Cindy was frantic. *Where could he be? Where did he go? I need to ask dad to find out. He knows all the right people.*

Cindy called her father at the office. His secretary answered.

"Hi, Miss Pringle. This is Cindy Stranton."

"Well, hi, Cindy. I hear you're making great progress and may be back with us in a couple of months."

"I hope so. Is my father there or is he busy?"

"Just a moment and I'll check. I'll connect you now."

"Hi, Dad."

"Well, hello sweetheart. It's good to hear your voice."

"I need a favor from you."

"Anything darling."

"I need to get in touch with Raymond, but he's nowhere to be found. Can you find out where he went?"

"Cindy, I wanted to tell you, but you were so angry that I didn't want to bring up his name until you were ready."

"Where is he, Dad?"

"He joined the Army the day after you sent him away."

Cindy bit her lip and started to tremble. Tears rolled down her cheeks. "Thanks, daddy." She slowly put the phone down.

Now what am I going to do without him?

When her parents arrived that evening, Cindy decided to reveal her secret. She was tactful in defining her love for Raymond and explaining that the baby was conceived out of their loving relationship.

"I've decided to have the baby and raise it myself. When the war is over and Raymond returns, we'll get married and everything will end well."

Mr. and Mrs. Stranton looked at each other speechless. They both showed concern that Cindy's plans might not work out.

"Are you sure you don't want to give the baby up for adoption? You were very angry with Raymond when he left."

"No, mother, I made a mistake. I love Raymond and I want his baby. I know it will be hard, but I can do it with help."

Lucille thought, *How will I explain to my friends at the club that Cindy is having a baby out of wedlock? We'll be the talk of the town.*

"Since you're keeping the child, couldn't we say that you and Raymond married secretly before he left for the service?"

"I don't think anyone would believe that lie. Although, I will buy a ring to wear until our wedding day."

Seven months later, Cindy delivered a baby boy named Robert, after his father. A ten-day hospital stay was mandatory for Cindy, but she walked out of the facility with only a slight limp and a prognosis of a complete recovery. She started to take on a few cases at the law firm, but didn't overload herself with work, so more time was spent with her son. Cindy gave up her apartment and moved back to the Grand Concourse. Returning home enabled Robert to receive extra attention from his grandparents. Cindy used her old bedroom while her son's nursery was in the room Daryl used growing up. Robert's crib, bassinet, and layette were set up before he came home. Eventually, a nanny was hired, and Cindy returned to work full-time. She took her mother's advice and bought a wedding band, telling everyone they married before Raymond enlisted.

Since Cindy learned that Raymond was a soldier, she followed the progression of the war on radio and reading newspapers even more carefully. The media never provided enough information so Cindy lacked knowledge of Raymond's whereabouts.

Out of fear and loneliness, Cindy became overwhelmed with the need to write Raymond about their son, grant him forgiveness and say, "I'll be waiting." *Where is he stationed? I can picture him marching throughout Europe and fighting the Nazis. How many people did he kill or capture?*

It was late summer of 1943 when Cindy picked up the phone to call Raymond's parents: They represented the only connection to him. She hadn't spoken to them since the engagement, which seemed an eternity ago. When Mr. Miller picked up the phone and said, "Hello," Cindy felt embarrassed and tongue-tied. *What do you say to the father of the son you sent away to war and now want back?*

"Mr. Miller, this is Cindy Stranton."

"Oh, Cindy. Are you fully recuperated from the accident?"

"Yes, sir. I'm back to work full-time. Mr. Miller, I need to know where to write Raymond."

"He was working on becoming a prominent lawyer when you sent him away. What do you want from him now?"

"I know. I'm sorry, but I was out-of-my-mind with pain and fearful of losing control of my body. I could have died. If he had been honest with me from the beginning, this mess might never have happened."

"Well, Cindy, you're too late. Corporal Donavan, from Battalion 570, informed me by letter that Private Raymond Miller, Jr. is missing in action. He landed by parachute in enemy territory somewhere in the foothills of Germany last week during a clandestine mission."

Choked with emotion, he continued in a solemn tone: "I'm using my influence in Washington to have Raymond tracked down and brought home, but it might be futile. I won't give up until I see his body dead or alive. I'm sorry, Miss Stranton; right now I can't help you and maybe I never will be able to."

Cindy gave her sympathies and said, "Goodbye." She felt heartsick. Her body shook from the feeling of abandonment. She picked up the picture frame on her desk and stared at the two of them celebrating their engagement at the Persian House. *How could our lives have turned so sour after such a binding commitment? Maybe having the baby was a wrong decision. Robert might never know his father. My dearest might never return to me.*

A cry from Robert's room broke Cindy's trance. She went to investigate his problem. Cindy turned the light on and found a sleepy one-year-old with tousled sandy-blond hair, dimpled chin, and frightened hazel eyes.

"What's the matter, sweetie?"

"Mommy, mommy!"

"You scared? I'm scared too, my darling, baby boy."

At that moment, Cindy knew she couldn't live without her son. Robert wore Raymond's face. She went over and hugged the child. "Don't be frightened, my son; together we'll survive, one day at a time."

Raymond gave up on surviving as he hovered in the corner of his damp, cold, four-by-four cell. Blinded by darkness, Raymond sat trying to figure out the location of his captivity. He remembered descending from the aircraft and landing on a gravel road near a dense forest. As he scrambled to his feet and rid himself of his bulky parachute, he went for his map to find the location where his platoon from Special Forces was hiding. It was too late. Five Nazis came out of the woods, one yelling in English, "Throw down your gun and backpack." The German soldiers aimed their bayonets at his heart. Raymond figured, *No*

use fighting, I'm outnumbered, and unfamiliar with the territory.
He placed his hands behind his head and surrendered.

If Raymond knew of the torture that awaited him, his decision to attempt escape and possibly be shot was a better alternative. His rations were moldy bread and polluted water. He had the runs and the cell reeked. With no food in his belly and frequent blows to his head, Raymond knew he would be dead soon. The Nazi Captain, Frederick Heimlich, thought he was lying when he said he had no information about his mission other then to be prepared to attack Berlin.

"How many men? Tell me the day, and time of the bombings," the captain kept hammering at him. The cigarette burns on his arms, and the open cuts on his back from beatings told the story of his pain. His memory started to fade. He remembered the girl he left behind, but now he couldn't remember her name. *One more torture session will be my demise,* he thought. Raymond's hopes of being found by his battalion seemed lost.

Then he heard the roar of engines. Planes flew low overhead and bullets tore into the ground. He wondered, *Is this my rescue—or—death?* He scrambled to his feet and started shouting, "I'm here! I'm here!" No answer. He went back and curled up into a fetal position. He saw the beady yellow eyes of the rats ready to attack his dead flesh. Daybreak came. He heard footsteps. With all his strength, he took his dirty dented tin cup and banged the metal bars: "I'm here." He could hardly spill out the words from lack of food, water, and breath. Was it friend or foe? He didn't care. *Just get me out of this cage. Kill me now or set me free.* As he looked up to learn his fate, he saw the badge of stars and stripes on the soldier's shirt.

CHAPTER 34

▼

NEW BEGINNINGS

Packing all day long, with boxes placed everywhere, moving was for the strong and Becky's health was fragile, which made her vulnerable to exhaustion. But she was persistent and used her patience like a bear getting ready for hibernation. She sat and wrapped all her clean breakables, first in paper towel, to protect them from the black ink in the newspaper that she used as added protection. The girls pitched in with packing their own precious items. Mom advised, "Give away old games and books. You've outgrown them and storage is limited in a no-basement house."

Out went Dena's movie star collection, Archie comic books, and Nancy Drew mysteries. She kept telling herself, *I'm a teenager. Soon I'll learn to drive; I don't need these things*, but she cringed when depositing them at the Salvation Army.

Although excitement was in the air, the Abroms had anxiety about leaving a neighborhood that they lived in for nineteen years. For Dena, it was fourteen. Aunt Mary died before she graduated from Durfee Junior High, but it was hard leaving her sister, Dottie, and the memorable Sunday dinners of bagels and salami sandwiches, fancy salads, and ice cream with chocolate chip cookies, all eaten while watching *The Ed Sullivan Show*.

Rena said, "Hooray. Finally, I get my own bedroom. I deserved it at age twenty-two." She had no attachment to the old neighborhood and Rena left no friends behind. *Taking two buses to work will be a pain, but nothing is perfect,* Rena thought.

The United Van Lines truck pulled up onto the driveway one week after graduation in June, 1956. Becky worried that if it rained, the men would bring mud into the new house with their wet shoes. In fact, it was a bright hot day for the end of June and all they thought about was keeping cool and drinking enough water. Loading and unloading the valuables took all day, but finding a place for everything was harder than packing.

Nate received a rude awaking one evening, when a polo game was scheduled. The band blared music as he tried to sleep before work. He ended up putting cotton in his ears.

"Becky, I'll be glad when they move and peace and quiet returns."

The girls thought it was a cool experience. Where else could they get all this action outside their front door?

Each girl had adjustments. Dena thought hers was the hardest. No alleys existed like on Monterey where she could meet kids and play baseball and school didn't start for another two months. She called old friends, but she needed her father for transportation to their house. By September, she was ready for high school even if the experience frightened her. In Durfee, she was popular and knew practically everyone. At Redford High School, she was going in cold, not knowing a soul. The Five Points bus came every hour on the hour, so if she missed it, she had to walk a mile to catch the Seven Mile bus to Grand River and walk a couple of blocks to the school. On the first day, Dena approached the monster-size building and stared. She was scared. Redford's new addition made it look large and frightening. She received her class schedule and tried to locate the rooms, but they were scattered and on different levels. *I'm going to be late to my classes trying to figure this mess out.* Discouraged, she thought, *Should I throw in the towel and run home? That wouldn't help matters.* She asked two girls standing in the hall, who looked friendly, to guide her to most of the classes. After that ordeal, it was smooth sailing. Friends came easily and she started enjoying being a freshman. One fast lesson: Rosedale Park girls and sorority sisters were out of her league. They came from money.

Another obstacle for Dena to overcome was dating. Becky wouldn't let her date until she was fifteen years old and they had to be Jewish boys. *Well, what a predicament,* Dena thought. *We live in a school district where only one percent of Jews attend this school and mother places demands on me.* Dena felt trapped and silly when giving excuses as to why she couldn't accept a date. She stuck to activities with girlfriends. She cruised on Grand River, went to Redford football games or acted silly at pajama parties. She babysat once a week to keep extra money in her pocket. On weekdays, Dena rushed home from school to watch Dick Clark's *American Bandstand* at 4:00 o'clock.

The only complaint that Rena had about the new house was being stranded out in the boonies. She loved walking to the neighborhood movies or taking a bus downtown to the Fox or United Artists theatre. They were all waiting for Dena to get her driver's license to go places, but Rena had choices now. She could take a bus to Northland Mall on Eight Mile, a bus to the Avenue of Fashion as Livernois was called or take two buses, with well over an hour of traveling time, to go downtown. Ferguson's, on the Avenue of Fashion, was her favorite place to shop and she discovered the Redford Theatre near Dena's school.

Once in a while, Rena was fixed up on a blind date, but she thought the guys were "schmos" and decided she would rather sit home and listen to her record albums then go out with jerks.

CHAPTER 35

▼

TOPPER

Making close friends wasn't Rena's forté. So she needed a companion to fill the void—man's best friend, a dog. How was she going to convince finicky Becky on the idea? Rena pleaded and gave her sales pitch: "The dog will be my responsibility. I'll pay for his shots, fed him, train him, and clean up after him."

After a lot of thinking, Becky must have concluded that a pet would benefit Rena and agreed, but not without conditions.

"Rena, you can have your dog, but it must stay outdoors in a doghouse. I don't want doggie hair or a doggie smell inside."

Rena researched for a breed that would be suited for those conditions and concluded that a Sheltie would be a perfect outdoor pet. She looked in the classified ads of the newspaper for a breeder located close to Detroit.

On a Sunday morning in June, 1957, Rena and Nate drove out to Parker's Kennel located just outside Ann Arbor in

Chelsea, Michigan. When they arrived, Rena jumped out of the car and ran toward the puppies' location. She stepped inside their kennel and one came toward her and jumped and twirled around. She fell in love with it. "This is the one I must have. The little brown and white furball with big brown eyes and a playful disposition is so cute." Mrs. Parker took the puppy and placed him in a box to make traveling easier for Nate and Rena and gave her the papers identifying his pedigree.

Dena couldn't wait until they came home so she could see her sister's selection. Rena placed the box in the utility room, where the puppy would stay until he was old enough to live outside. Everyone gathered around the dog commenting on how cute he was. Dena asked, "What is the dog's name?"

"I'm going to call him Topper."

"Why 'Topper'?"

"Because when I saw him, he jumped up and down and around like a top."

When it was time for Topper to make his home outside, Rena purchased a big white doghouse that was placed in the back of the yard. Topper loved his new home. He had plenty of room to run around in a cyclone-fenced yard. Topper, however, didn't watch out for Nate's flower garden as he ran back and forth barking, and he trampled on the beautiful blooms. Nate took care of that situation by putting up a fenced dog run.

Topper was loved and played with in the fall, and in spring and summer he was allowed on the screened porch to play when the family was sitting outside. Rena swept out the hair after Topper's visits. However, it was the long Michigan winters that spelled trouble. Rena gave him his food, but play was limited. Dena was too busy going out with her boyfriend to pay much attention. Nate was working and had limited time and Becky's health wasn't up to caring for a dog. So when Rena started to travel and began going out, Topper became a problem. He was cared for but not given enough attention.

It was in the spring, after having Topper for three years, that the family noticed him being more aggressive in his play. He wasn't acting friendly toward the girls.

"That's odd," remarked Rena.

Dena commented, "Maybe he's lonely and needs a family with young kids that will play with him all the time."

Sadly, Rena admitted that Dena was right. Rena advertised in the newspaper and within a week, a young woman with two children came to pick Topper up. The Abrom family was sorry to see him go, but knew it was in the best interest of the dog.

CHAPTER 36

▼

GROWN-UP

Spring of 1957 arrived and Dena decided it was time to change her dating dilemma. A Mumford High School friend, Joan Adler, called:

"Dena, the Synagogue on Evergreen and Seven Mile has a youth group. This Sunday, a member is having a house party. Let's go."

"OK. I'll ask my dad if he can drive me to your house, and we'll go together." A few hours before getting together, Joan called to say she wasn't feeling well. "I'm sorry, but count me out."

Dena thought: *What do I do now?* Quickly, she decided *If I can enter a new school with over a thousand students and not know a soul, I can go to this party alone.* Her mother, who worried about everything, encouraged her to go and meet some nice

Jewish kids. Nate drove Dena to the party and reaffirmed: "If you need a ride home, call and I'll pick you up."

"OK. Bye Dad."

She felt confident dressed in a straight calf-length navy skirt, topped with a powder-blue angora sweater resting below the waist, and dirty buck shoes. She entered the house and introduced herself to the hostess, Marilyn Siegel. Marilyn took her down to the basement where the party was in full swing. She started talking to some acquaintances, and noticed two fellows standing and drinking pop. *Boy, are they cute. I've got to meet them.* They just stood and talked, so Dena walked over and started a conversation.

"Do you go to Redford?"

Herb Light said, "Yes."

"I thought I saw you in the hall," she lied.

The other fellow, Marshall Neely, went to Mumford. Within the hour, they were ready to leave.

"Do you want to join us for pizza?" Herb asked. "I have my car."

She couldn't pass up the invitation. "Sure."

They went to Big Tony's Pizzeria on Seven Mile and when finished, they drove her home. When she entered her house and closed the door after thanking Herb, she yelled, "Mom, you won't believe what happened. I met the nicest two guys and both so good looking! I wonder if either one will call me."

Monday at school, she looked for Herb in the halls, but with no success. By the end of the week, she had heard from neither guy. Dena figured it was just wishful thinking. But Saturday morning, the doorbell rang.

"I'll get it, mother." To her surprise, there stood 6'4" Herb, *my movie star idols, Rock Hudson and Tony Curtis, all wrapped into one.* At that moment, Dena wished she was tall like her sister. In Durfee, the boys were shrimps and she wished to stay at 5'2". *Now,* she thought, *why did I wish so hard?* Becky came to the door and Dena introduced Herb to her. He shook her hand. She was impressed. They went for a ride to get acquainted. After that, they started dating. He turned sixteen in July and Dena was sweet sixteen in October. By seventeen they went steady. What impressed Dena about Herb was his work ethic. Before a date, they would stop so he could give estimates for laying tile on basement floors. One basement could run $200 to $300. He always had money in his pocket. He gave up the business when his knees became so sore from being on them too long. He started selling tile at a retail store. Not many 16-year-olds could go into Dexter Chevrolet and pay cash for a 1957 Impala. This reassured Dena that their future, if they married, could be financially bright. They wouldn't struggle like her Mom and Dad.

Becky wasn't prepared to deal with a teenager in love, especially a daughter who was going steady. Becky worried about their raging hormones. In the fifties, a good Jewish girl only necked or petted and didn't go further until marriage.

"Don't bring shame on the family," Becky kept telling her. They used to argue a lot about dating and curfews. Whatever her mother said was wrong. Becky hated to watch Dena smoke but it was cool in the fifties. She was afraid to say too much or Dena would yell at her and threaten to run away. Becky would lie in bed and cry. Nate was afraid his wife might have another breakdown. He said to Dena, "Be nicer to your mother and show some empathy."

"Mom forgot what it's like to be a teenager." Then she remembered that her mother was robbed of her adolescent years and couldn't relate.

Herb and Dena made plans. College was a must for him and Dena would get a job after graduating from high school. Although she wanted to go to college, her parents couldn't afford it.

"We'll take a loan out to send you to college, if you promise to finish and not drop out to get married," pressured mother.

She couldn't make that promise, as Herb and Dena wanted to get married when he finished at Wayne State University.

He remarked, "Why go to college? Eventually, we'll have a family and you won't be working anyway."

In the summer of 1959, Dena graduated and went to the prom wearing a long white organza strapless gown with green embroidery. Financially, the dress set Becky back two payments at Hudson's. Herb borrowed his boss's silver-gray Cadillac Eldorado convertible. They escaped into the fantasy of the wealthy for an evening. The next week, Dena started browsing the help wanted ads. Thank goodness, she had taken typing and bookkeeping in school along with a college curriculum. She went for the ad that read: "Need secretary and bookkeeper at fancy dress shop on the Avenue of Fashion." This was Dena's first job in retail and what a rude awakening. Her clothes came from department stores and Winkelman's. These clothes were couture fashion. They were something like Rena's taste, but Dena couldn't afford such extravagance, even with her discount.

She felt like a big shot earning $60 a week and paid $10 to her mother for room and board. Her sister had to pay that much. Like her sister, Dena had a goal she was saving towards. It wasn't traveling; it was buying herself a new car. Taking two buses to work in the winter wasn't her idea of fun. She wondered: *How did my dad travel that way for so long?* Dena saved and saved until she had enough for a down payment on a car. In 1960, she bought the first edition of the Ford Falcon for $2,036. She was so proud, and now became an additional driver in the family.

Excitement came when Dena was invited to accompany her boss, Mrs. Frandell, on a buying trip to New York. First time on a plane! First time on her own! That warranted buying her first two pieces of Samsonite luggage. She was feeling on top of the world, so when Herb proposed as soon as she turned nineteen, she was hesitant. Of course, romance won out. She wanted to be married and have her own place. It was time to leave the nest and that meant marriage. Dena and her mother became close again as they planned the wedding. They talked continuously about the preparations: band, flowers, pictures, food, and bridesmaids. Dena was going to have her bridal dress made by one of the seamstresses at Frandell's. The part that disappointed Dena the most was when her sister refused to be a bridesmaid. *I knew she was mad,* recalled Rena. I *didn't want everyone looking at me walking down the aisle and thinking I'm an old maid.*

Dena made two requests before their marriage could take place. First, her car would be paid in full. No wedding bliss with debt. Secondly, Herb must turn twenty-one, so no co-signing was needed to make large purchases. He agreed. There were some obstacles that were overlooked. Herb and Dena came from two different households. Dena's was organized, meticulous, and run by a homemaker. His mother worked full-time and ran the household in helter-skelter fashion. She was tall and strong, her movements quick, and no task too much. Becky was timid and weak and had nothing but time to complete a task. Diverse family environment can influence children beyond comprehension so many years of adjustment were necessary, but they weren't prepared for that part of the marriage. The commonality bond was their religion. All they knew was "love conquers all," and independence was their focus.

The rabbi expressed concern at their talk a month before the wedding.

"I think you're both too young and should wait a few years."

They took no heed. The big event took place two weeks after Herb's twenty-first birthday, on July 15, 1962. After a year of planning, the wedding took place in a synagogue. Nate walked Dena down the aisle to the song sung by Cantor Adler, "*Because.*" As she linked her arm into Herb's to walk under the Chuppa, Dena felt his arm shaking. She feared, *Is he afraid of this commitment? Was that a sign of a shaky future?*

An unexpected event took place about six months before Dena's wedding that was not in the planning, but made Becky very excited. A cousin fixed Rena up on a blind date and she was willing to go after much insistence by her mother. *I didn't want to go*, recalled Rena, *but mother harped so much I said, "Okay."* To everyone's surprise, she liked Jacob Fried and felt comfortable with him. The next week, he asked her out again and she agreed without any coaxing from Becky. They started dating and Jacob escorted her to Dena's wedding. The whole family started gossiping about the new beau in Rena's life. Six months later, Jacob popped the question and they were married in the rabbi's study followed by dinner with the immediate family at the Raleigh House. Becky didn't argue about the plans as she was broke and tired from the first wedding. Although Dena's wedding was modest and she helped her mother pay for the wedding, Becky needed to take out a small loan to pay the remaining bills.

Chapter 37

Next Generation

The first phase of Becky's job in life was completed with her daughters' marriages. She still participated by voicing her opinions and giving advice, but her responsibility of raising them ended and she felt a void in her life. It was peaceful in the house, but too peaceful. Loneliness set in and she couldn't stand the feeling of an empty house. "Nate, I no longer need a three-bedroom house to clean and maintain; let's sell and move into an apartment."

Nate hardly ever disagreed with his wife, but the decision was made in the late sixties when it became a buyers' market and they couldn't get the price they were asking. Instead of waiting, Becky let her emotions take over and they sold at a loss. Nate still worked his night shift and earned a good salary, so as their expenses for two people decreased they were able to save some money and feel secure.

The second phase of Becky's life began when she received the news that Dena was pregnant. After nine months of marriage, Becky's first granddaughter was born. What a surprise for Dena and Herb. They had no insurance for maternity costs, as the preexisting six months clause wasn't up. Herb still needed to take his C.P.A. exam, and Dena wanted to continue her career. They weren't prepared for their new roles. Becky was happy. Her daughter was married, her son-in-law a professional, and her biggest delight came from being a Bubbie, Yiddish for grandmother. Three years later, a second daughter was born.

The best-laid plans don't always work out. Dena needed an outlet. Staying home, cleaning, and caring for the girls wasn't enough. That's what Becky did, but Dena wanted more. She wanted to fulfill her dream and obtain a college education. She needed security in case her marriage didn't last. Herb was still growing up along with the girls. Dena was mature for her age, but still wet behind the ears and frustrated to boot. She never expressed these feelings to anyone except her closest friend, Barbara. Dena knew her parents would never understand. To them, raising a family made life complete. She knew her secretarial skills wouldn't bring in enough income if she and the girls were on their own. How was she to manage the house, the girls, and school?

She made the decision to take one class per semester in the evening at a community college until she earned sixty-four credit hours, transferable to a four-year college. Doing it alone wasn't feasible. Herb didn't complain about her plan but was too busy working to offer much help, but Bubbie and Pom, the grandkids nickname for grandpa, did. They babysat, chauffeured, and entertained their granddaughters when needed; no matter how many health issues, how busy or tired, they were available. When Dena called, they came. Becky didn't have time to focus on her ailments as her body started to deteriorate with aging, as she had a role to fulfill. In ten years, Dena earned a Bachelor of Arts Degree. Her proud family attended graduation to see her receive her hard-earned diploma. No one believed she would persevere. Ten years later, she received a Master's Degree in Social Work. How does a daughter give back to her parents in gratitude? By being their caregiver as they aged.

CHAPTER 38

▼

ADOPTION

Rena and Jacob wanted to start a family as Rena felt her biological clock was ticking away at thirty. Unfortunately, she couldn't get pregnant. After three years of trying, they decided to adopt. Through their attorney, they heard of a physician who had an unmarried patient ready to give up her baby. They were ecstatic about the news and told the lawyer to start making the arrangements. A court date was set for adoption proceedings. When the little girl was born, Jacob and Rena went to the hospital to visit and get acquainted with their baby. They went three times a week, but were afraid of becoming too attached in case something went wrong and they were denied the child. The family was investigated to evaluate if the Frieds would be appropriate parents and they had to complete many papers.

While waiting for the adoption to be finalized, Rena began to feel strange. She missed one period and felt sick to her stomach in the mornings. The thought of food made her ill. She wondered, *Could I possibly be pregnant?* She decided not to say a word until after next week's court date and they were approved to adopt the baby. She figured, *I can't give up this child that I held to my bosom for so many weeks. If the judge finds out I'm pregnant, he may stop the proceedings. I can't take that chance. What if I'm not pregnant or miscarry? Then I'll end up with nothing. I won't say anything, not even to Jacob or my family, until the baby is in our house. Then I'll go see a doctor.*

Rena and Jacob appeared before Judge Howell in September, 1968, just as the leaves scattered on the ground announcing that autumn was in the air. The Frieds answered the questions to the judge's approval. The child's mother released all maternal rights and the paperwork was completed correctly. Everything went like clockwork. Jacob and Rena were presented with their bundle of joy and walked out of the courthouse, a family of three.

Eight months later, Rena gave birth to another little girl. Was it difficult with two infants? Of course; but her parents were there to help. Becky's second phase in life, caring for the grandchildren, became as important as caring for her own children. But it was different. She loved them but could return them to their parents. Instead of being harsh and strict like when raising her own family, she turned into a kind, gentle grandparent with the patience to focus on their care. The grandchildren adored their Bubbie Becky and Pom and looked forward to being with them. Not only did they help both daughters with their children's care, but they babysat when the parents went on vacation.

This was their life and this was what made them feel young and happy. They rehashed their family's success even without having much money. Both daughters married husbands of their own faith and there were four granddaughters to continue the lineage. Rena enjoyed the role of motherhood and was content staying home like her mother did. As her children grew older, Rena depended less on her parents for help. However, she vowed the same as Dena that they would never feel alone and somehow or someway she would pay them back in the future. That time came when they aged.

CHAPTER 39

▼

REUNITED WITH IRENA

Becky felt pressure on her chest and sporadic pain throughout the day, but didn't want to believe anything was wrong. She checked her watch and said to Nate, "Oh, no. I have a hair appointment at 1:00 this afternoon."

"You're not going the way you feel."

"Of course I'm going. I'll be fine."

As Nate drove to Suzie's Salon, Becky explained, "I bet it's acid reflux from that darn bleeding ulcer caused by too many aspirins all these years. Tomorrow I have an appointment with Dr. Lossman. I'll let him know my symptoms."

The pain still persisted as she waited in the examining room. Dr. Lossman raised his eyebrows as Becky described her discomfort.

"Give Mrs. Abrom in room three an EKG," he ordered his nurse. After reading the results, he looked alarmed. He called Mr. Abrom into the room.

"My receptionist is calling for an ambulance. You need to get to Sinai Hospital, immediately. Mrs. Abrom, you had a heart attack and need medical attention."

Becky was placed in intensive care for a week and monitored by a cardiologist. She remained in Sinai another two weeks. Nitroglycerin kept the angina stabilized. While in bed, she wondered, *How did I get a heart attack at sixty-five? Could it be from enduring so many losses as a youngster, the stress of raising teenagers, planning weddings, or holding up during the birth of grandchildren? No, it's the accumulation of pain that took a toll on my heart or maybe years of financial woes.* Then she remembered her father's first heart attack when he was in his sixties. *I need some life changes.* She vowed to lose weight and try exercising without hurting her legs.

But she couldn't ignore the increased pain in her right leg. Dr. Richman's surgery had kept her going for twenty years. Now, the inflammation was back and the redness around the patch had intensified.

"Nate, I need to see the orthopedic surgeon. Maybe some new methods came into effect regarding grafting."

However, when Dr. Richman looked at Becky's leg, he looked grim.

"Honestly, Mrs. Abrom, the only way I can tell what's going on underneath is with surgery to lift the grafted patch."

Without hesitation, Becky answered, "I know when to leave well enough alone. If you do surgery, I might not heal and I'd end up in a wheelchair."

"That's a possibility. One caveat: If you fall and break your leg or hip, I can't promise to put you back together. Treat your leg carefully. As you age, your bones become brittle and can just snap."

Again, the doctor offered a prescription for morphine for pain, but Becky refused. This time Extra Strength Tylenol became her friend. It was gentler on her stomach.

Becky left his office feeling down-in-the dumps over the medical assessment. So, when the phone rang and the unfamiliar voice asked, "Is this the Abrom household?" Becky perked up.

"I'm looking for a Becky Abrom."

"This is she and who are you?"

"You may not remember me, but my name is Irena Collins."

"Are you my niece, Irena, from California?"

"I don't know. That's what I called to find out." Irena explained her story.

"I'm getting married and planning a honeymoon in Europe. I needed a passport and had to know my mother's maiden name. I went through papers looking for this information and found my birth certificate that stated my mother was Lilly Hooberman. I was shocked. I never heard that name before. I called my dad and he explained what happened to my biological mother and how I was raised by my stepmother. Now I'm trying to find my family roots and learn about my mother and her family. My aunt Karen told me about my mother's sister, Becky, and her brother Jake. She found your number and passed it on. Aunt Becky, I'd love to meet you, but I can't make the trip to Detroit. I can't take time off from work."

"I want to see you again, Irena. You are the link to my Lilly. Let me see what I can do."

Becky took her number and said goodbye. Becky was excited as she related the story to Nate.

"I can't believe, after all this time, I can meet Lilly's daughter all grown up."

"Don't get your hopes up too high, Becky."

She quickly called Dena to tell her of the conversation. The last memory Dena had of her cousin was when Irena was brought over the house to say goodbye. They were playing a board game and Irena wasn't winning, so she tipped over the whole game. *I wonder what she's like now*, thought Dena.

Nate was still working at age seventy-eight and wasn't planning retirement. The longer he stayed employed, the higher his Social Security check would be when he did retire. However, the police stopped him one night. They thought he was drunk, as his car weaved across the road. He explained to the officers that he had just gotten off work and was exhausted. He must have dozed for a minute. When Becky heard the story and saw the ticket, she insisted that he retire immediately. Enough was said; he ended his career.

Now that Nate had retired after a month's notice, the decision was made that Dena and her daughter Stella were going to take Becky and Nate to California to meet Irena. Dena couldn't remember her parents ever going on a trip. Dena loved California and thought taking her parents for this reunion would boost her mother's morale as well as celebrate her father's retirement.

When Dena approached her parents with this idea, they agreed, but Dena had one condition: "Mom, you will need a wheelchair. You can't walk the distance either at the airport or sightseeing."

To her surprise, her mother agreed. "Okay. I realize I can't do all that walking anymore."

Dena was shocked. *Boy*, she thought, *mother must really want to reunite with Irena if she agreed without an argument.* Dena had some apprehension. *What if Irena looked exactly like Lilly and Becky got emotionally enmeshed with her niece? How would my parents deal with flying? It would be a first for both.*

"I'll call United Airlines to reserve bulkhead seats for us," she told her mother. "I'm also going to buy a little stool to put out once the plane is in the air, so you can elevate your leg."

"Hum," said Becky. "You think of everything."

Becky and Nate were excited about their trip. Becky was packed a week ahead of time and the plans were in place. There was no problem at the airport and Nate loved flying and being among people. California was inhabited by young people, out and about in the warm weather. Becky and Nate had the time of their life in the hotel, sightseeing, eating out at restaurants, visiting shopping malls, and visiting with Irena. She was so cordial and gave plenty of attention to her newly-found aunt and uncle. Dena was pleasantly surprised. At Irena's house they went over pictures and she had one of her mother, Lilly. It happened Lilly looked like Dena. *Maybe that's why mother depends on me so much*, she thought. After the trip there were letters and promises which didn't last. Irena never came to Detroit to visit and meet her Uncle Jake as promised. He would have liked to make the connection, as he had acquired so much information about his niece, his link to the past. After the reunion with Irena, Becky found closure with Lilly's death and felt content.

Two years later, a strange episode occurred. Dena, Herb, and their girls, Laura and Stella, took a trip to California and made arrangements to see Irena. Before the planned gathering, Herb and the girls were walking on the beach, while Dena went to meet an old acquaintance at a restaurant. They ran into Irena and her husband jogging. Stella recognized them and yelled "Hi!" excited to see her cousin. But Irena wouldn't stop. She just yelled back, "Hi! We'll see you tonight."

However, the meeting never happened. Irena called to cancel the plans at the last minute. She was never seen or heard from again. When the family discussed what had transpired, they couldn't believe her indifference. Dena just shook her head and shrugged her shoulders: "Well, I guess our rekindled relationship just ended."

When they came home and related the story to Becky, it didn't matter to her. She already had peace of mind.

CHAPTER 40

▼

EPILOGUE

Edger Allan Poe wrote, "We loved with a love that was more than love—I and my Annabel Lee." Or, as Nate put it, "I and my Becky."

His devotion never faltered all through their fifty-six years of marriage. He could have shirked his responsibilities after the accident, but that wasn't his nature. Becky was his love and support. He protected and cared for her no matter how many challenges they encountered. Work and dedication to his family were Nate's accomplishments. Some people might find it menial. To Becky, he was her savior. To his girls, he was their idol. To Nate, they completed his life.

Raymond chose to run. His young recklessness changed a family's life. No ties—no looking back. No devotion to anyone but himself. Did he use his second chance wisely? Each individual can decide his worth. After he caused damage to the second woman, Cindy, supposedly his love, Raymond chose to run again. He claimed it was his patriotic duty, not an escape. The war may have changed his life. The facts are unknown. His outcome, maybe, was his judgment.

Before his death, Nate saved Becky one last time. Two years after his retirement, Nate, at eighty, was diagnosed with Parkinson's disease. The progression of decreased muscle tone, mobility, and mental status came slowly, but within five years, he needed a lot of care. Becky refused to place him in a nursing home.

"He took care of me all these years, paid the bills, and never discarded me like yesterday's newspaper," she told her family. "I will keep him with me."

She hobbled around to dress, bathe, and cook for him. She never left his side. Being a caregiver is never easy, especially for a handicapped person. The wear and tear on Becky's body caused her health to deteriorate. The family helped, but the burden remained hers. It became a question of who would die first.

It happened on a sunny summer day with the flowers in full bloom, Nate's favorite time of year. He went to speak to Becky and his speech was gibberish. Alarmed, she called EMS. They took him to the hospital where he underwent a full examination. Within a few hours his speech returned. They determined he had experienced a TIA, a Transit Ischemic Attack or ministroke. The doctor wanted to keep him for 24-hour observation. The family agreed. When Dena came to pick him up the next day, he wasn't dressed. When she went to help him, he screamed in pain. Dena ran for a nurse. The RN reported, "Mr. Abrom fell out of bed earlier."

"Was he X-rayed?"

"Well—no."

"How can the doctor discharge a patient who fell out of bed without X-raying for a fracture? I want him X-rayed immediately."

Within the hour, Dr. Nelson and staff came to Nate's room with the results and an apology. "You have every right to be upset, Mrs. Light. Your father has a fractured hip and we scheduled surgery for tomorrow."

A week later, he was transferred to a nursing home for rehabilitation. Yet, more was on Nate's mind than walking. He knew his wife could no longer care for him, but would insist on taking him home anyway. To spare her, he just gave up. Two weeks later, he died of pneumonia. Becky's grieving took its toll, but she trudged on. For Nate's efforts of working thirteen years beyond retirement age, she received enough Social Security to move into an independent senior residence.

Becky's coping mechanism enabled her to outlive most of her elderly family members and friends. Through life's painful journey, she reaped bountiful rewards. She saw four granddaughters married and four great-grandchildren born.

The turning point came eleven years after her husband's death. After firing all the help Dena had hired, Becky fell in her apartment one evening. It wasn't the first time; in fact, she had fallen too many times to count. This time, however, she couldn't get up and was too far away from the pull cord to ring for assistance. She stayed on the floor all night until the physical therapist found her in the morning. Did she do the unthinkable, what Dr. Richman warned her about? Did she break any bones? The ambulance took her to the hospital's emergency room. She was examined and X-rayed. All bones intact—a miracle for someone who had such bad arthritis and osteoporosis. However, it became too dangerous for her to live alone. Becky spent her last two-and-a-half years in a nursing home confined to a wheelchair. On one of Dena's visits to see her mother, she noticed the look of frustration and discouragement.

"Mom, are you tired of living this way?"

Becky looked cross and answered, "God saved my life sixty-five years ago and kept me going for a reason. I will never give up living until he decides to take me. Then, it will be my time."

Her time came at age eighty-five.

Although Becky never knew the drunk driver, Raymond Miller, Jr., she never found it in her heart to forgive that person. She always possessed bitterness towards the perpetrator for destroying her chance for a normal life. Due to a light stroke and mild dementia, however, Becky stopped rehashing that devastating day in 1935 and acquired a passive acceptance.

ABOUT THE AUTHOR

Doreen Lichtman started her career as a social worker late in life. It took nine years for her to earn a Bachelor of Arts degree from Wayne State University in Detroit, Michigan, while raising two daughters. During the next ten years she worked part-time in property management, while assisting her aging parents. Foreseeing an increase in the older population and their need for services, Lichtman returned to college to earn a Master's Degree in Social Work from University of Michigan and a certificate from the Institute of Gerontology in Ann Arbor.

In the following years, her tasks as caregiver increased, but she felt comfortable in the role since Lichtman's experience started at an early age. Her mother had suffered the aftermath from being hit by a drunk driver before Lichtman's birth. She grew up with a mother who always suffered ill-health. Through the years, Doreen's mother repeated the stories of her misfortune and told her daughter to write a book someday about the tragedy and the toll it took on the family.

Five years after her mother's death, Lichtman began her painful journey into the past and completed her first book, "Survival From Malice," in December 2003. She added a twist to her mother's story by letting her imagination develop the character of the hit-and-run driver and his fate.

Although Lichtman retired from Botsford General Hospital in Farmington Hills, Michigan, as medical social worker in the rehabilitation unit, she remains an advocate for seniors and caregivers. She is a certified leader for the Arthritis Foundation Self-Help Course. Doreen belongs to the Geriatric Social Workers and National Association of Social Workers Organizations.

She makes her home in Orchard Lake, Michigan, a suburb of Detroit.

References

Barfknecht, Gary, W. Mich.-Again's Day. C. 1984. Friede Publications, 1-18-43. Pgs. 11, 26,108, 135, 143.

Batterberry, Michael and Arlene. On The Town in New York. From 1776 to the Present. C. 1973. Charles Scribner's Sons, New York. Pgs. 220-270.

Feinman, Jay, M. Law 101. Everything You Need to Know About the American Legal System. Oxford, New York. C. 2000. Pgs. 158-161.

Loftus, John and Aarons, Mark. The Secret War Against The Jews. St. Martin's Press. C. 1994. Pgs. 8-27.

Reisman, John, M. DePaul University, A History of Clinical Psychology. Irvington Publishers, Inc., New York. C. 1976. Pgs. 35-242.

Stevens, Rosemary. In Sickness and in Wealth: American Hospitals in The Twentieth Century. New York: Basic Books, (Non-profit). C. 1989. Pgs. 82-170.

Uschan, Michael, V. A Cultural History of the United States Through the Decades. Lucent Books. San Diego, California. Pgs. 9-36.

Websites

BCBSM-Corporate History. Highlights of Our History 1929-
   1969. Retrieve4-15-03.Website:
   http://www.bcbs.com/blues/about/hist.shtml.C. 1996-2003.
   Pgs. 1-4.

Capuano, Deborah. (1998) Healthtouch-Spinal Cord Injury
   Treatment and Rehabilitation. Retrieved 9-29-03, from
   Transverse Myelitis Club List. Website:
   http://www. myelitis. Org/time/archive/18/0506.html. Pgs.
   1-8.

DeLang, Bradford, J. of University of California. A Study of the
   Economics of The Great Depression. Retrieved 12-10-03. A
   Brief History of Helen Hayes Hospital. Retrieved 9-29-03
   from Helen Hayes Hospital History: 1900-2001. Website:
   http://www.helenhayeshospital.org/hist.htm. Pgs. 1-3.

Techner, David. The Jewish Funeral-A Celebration of Life.
   Retrieved 2-23-02.Website:
   http://www.biomed.lib.umn.edu/hw/jewish.html. Pgs. 1-3.

978-0-595-36593-7
0-595-36593-0

Printed in the United States
47715LVS00003B/196-279

9 780595 365937